# Double Wahala, Double Trouble

UCHECHUKWU PETER UMEZURIKE

Griots Lounge Publishing
Canada

Published in 2021 by

Griots Lounge Publishing Canada
www.griotslounge.ca
Email: info@griotslounge.ca

DOUBLE WAHALA, DOUBLE TROUBLE

Library and Archives Canada Cataloguing in Publication

ISBN: 978-1-7776884-0-0

Cover Art by Fred Martins
Interior Design by Rachelle Painchaud-Nash

Printed and bound in Canada

# CONTENTS

# TRAVELLING WITH
## *DOUBLE WAHALA, DOUBLE TROUBLE*

i.

Stories are mobile. A story is remarkably mobile, hardly static. When I start writing a story, I don't know what route it will take, where it might lead, and what it might find along its path. Sometimes, a story strays a little too far off the road I've already mapped. I try not to fidget when this happens. If anything, I'm pleasantly surprised to see a story detouring, skirting a road-block, exploring new tracks—or even burrowing through the undergrowth to uncover wonders. Who is not cheered by the pleasure of unique finds!

ii.

Other times, a story springs with vigour and charges like a bull only to bump into a dead-end, flopping to the tar. I've seen it stall, refractory as a camel at rest—kick its underside as hard as you can, but it never budges. Such stories cause me to fret, though only momentarily. I have learned to tarry, waiting, hopeful as ever. Stories may stall, as indeed they should, but they are never, ever inert.

iii.

Stories are geographies, a journey of a kind, an inroad into the reader's heart. Stories travel. That is the wonder of it all—stories do travel. Stories travel with us, just as we travel with stories. The stories in *Double Wahala, Double Trouble* have travelled far and wide with me, from Africa to North America, Europe, and Asia. Most of them bear some semblance to several travellers I've met on sundry journeys. I've tried to reproduce peculiar encounters, and I can only hope that readers find something resonant about these stories, can recreate their own journeys into the world that I've attempted to delineate.

iv.

Perhaps, all I have tried to do in the collection is to track our proclivities for love and hate, intimacy and violence, fidelity and treachery. *Double Wahala, Double Trouble* maps stories of messiness, of fragilities and vulnerabilities of what we claim is humanity in a world doggedly inequitable.

# FLESH OF MY FLESH

Daluchi remembers him drunk. A breathless, grasping figure. She remembers the way her heart lifted, the very night she brought Tobe home after his younger brother had kicked him out. She had rescued a stray soul. She finds it endearing, the look in his small brown eyes, the look of an innocent frail man, the wounded look he gives her when he tries to snuggle up against her. But that expression has been missing for months. Still, he touches a spot between her breasts, leaving a flutter there, as if his fingertip is tracing her navel.

Tobe is telling her about a catfish he saw on his way home from the bottling factory where he works, somewhere around MCC Road. The fish is the length of his arm. Daluchi only buys roasted or fried fish. But he had purchased a live catfish and grilled it for her one Saturday evening when the wind had charged up and rattled the roofs of buildings in the neighbourhood, chasing everyone off the street. Despite her protests, he held her hands, tightening her grasp around the knife, and made her gut the writhing creature.

It was the first time Daluchi had killed a fish. As she sliced the soft, quivery belly, she felt like the knife was cutting slices off her. Her skin crawled. The sharp, greasy smell scratched her throat. She tried not to vomit. Tobe had watched her, a satisfied glint in his eyes the whole time. She hated the way he laughed—showing the inside of his mouth and beer-stained teeth—at her puckered face while she washed the reddish-orange eggs off her fingers.

"I wish I had bought that fish," says Tobe.

Daluchi frowns and notices a tear on the couch, which she will have to fix.

He sees the swaddled finger on her left hand. "What happened?"

*How else could I show him now that I'd do anything for him?*

Daluchi stops herself from grinding her teeth. Her head buzzes from the pain in her swaddled finger, but she tells herself to endure it.

"Anything," she says, feeling quite dizzy.

He creases his brow. "I don't understand."

*He wouldn't. How convenient. The man he is today, she made him. Turned her own frog into a prince.*

"Have you taken any medicine?"

"Not yet." Daluchi sees his face contort and adds, "I will."

Tobe rubs her back. "When did this happen?"

*Does he know what lengths I would go to keep him?*

She regrets not taking painkillers to lessen the burning in her hand. Fighting off the dizziness, she sighs. "Love is sacrifice."

Her response deepens the puzzled expression on his face. He now looks as though he's bashed his head against the door. And he had, once, when he stumbled home drunk and tripped in the doorway.

"I'm sorry," he murmurs, scratching his nose. "It's been a busy day." He rests his head on her shoulder and shuts his eyes for a moment.

She longs to stroke his earlobe with her right hand, but she changes her mind and keeps it resting on the armrest.

A motorcycle growls outside the window, and a dog starts yapping at something. It is past six, though the sun is still creeping around in the sky. Children shout and squeal in the street—their delight so easy, so unsullied, Daluchi finds it annoying. She wonders what their parents are doing right now.

*How convenient that they allow their children to bound from one house to another like mongrels, not minding that a car had all but run a child over before.*

*Maybe they're breeding more babies, again, as Tobe would joke.*

Late one evening, the children had invaded the street, screaming and running after each other. Their crazy game had driven Tobe to a fit, but there was nothing he could do about it. He merely complained to her about how wild they were, how their parents were busy competing to see who amongst themselves would produce the most babies. It would get to a point, he predicted, that parents would use their children for fencing their houses. He added that the more children a mother had, the less attention she gave them. She wound up becoming less emotionally attached to her flock. Daluchi found the jokes distasteful because she dreamt of being a mother herself. Tobe had never thought very highly of his mother.

The squeals grow louder in the street—their pitch maddening. Daluchi considers racing to the window to shush the children. She decides to endure the din, not wanting any foul-mouthed mother to remind her that she has yet to have a child of her own.

"You should have seen the fish," Tobe says, glancing up at her. A wistful smile spreads across his face.

The fish talk bores her, chafes her a little, so she changes the subject. "I prepared your favourite meal."

"You did?" He sits up, sniffs the air.

"Guess what it is?"

"Mmm-hmm." He walks to the window, still smiling.

The memory of the fish Tobe had seen might still be dancing in his mind. Daluchi purses her lips, thinking how small he looks. She's a foot taller than him, and his chinos usually bunch around his ankles. Longer pants enhance his height, she knows.

*What did I even see in him?*

"Come here," Tobe whispers, without turning around. He holds his hand out to her. "See?"

*Is he going to make fun of the children, as usual?*

She gets up and goes to stand next to him.

The warm evening air touches her cheeks. The horizon, wreathed in orange and purple, reminds her of a film where two lovers sit on a sand dune and gaze into the wildfire sunset. While she and Tobe had been watching the movie, he'd wrapped his arms around her like he wouldn't ever let go.

Daluchi doesn't take his hand. "See what?"

"There." He points at the old woman in a faded white top limping along on crutches toward the road. She is wearing one of those cheap T-shirts advertising a politician's oily face, the type that thugs hand out during election campaigns.

A tricycle appears from nowhere and screeches abruptly, missing the woman by a fraction. The impact is still powerful enough to cause her to crumple into a heap on the curb. Her crutches fly off her hands. A girl standing on the veranda lets out a long, piercing cry. Tobe swears, snapping his fingers. Daluchi gasps and clings to his body.

The old woman now sits on the ground, her legs splayed in front of her. She begins to fume, barely traumatized. She doesn't hug herself in shock or tremble from her close contact with death. Pedestrians have gathered around her, chattering and casting glances at one another.

A boy points to the distance, saying, "Look! It went that way. It went that way."

But the vehicle with its yellow and black stripes has long vanished.

"That's how people die," Tobe muses aloud, rubbing Daluchi's shoulder.

Accidents happen in the neighbourhood from time to time, but they still leave Daluchi shaken. She began feeling like this after the cat incident. One afternoon in September, she'd been sitting on the veranda watching a pregnant cat slink across the road. A car had shot out of the blue and crushed the animal to a bloodied pulp. The accident happened a year ago, but the image of that cat occasionally floods her brain.

"I hope Amadioha strikes him," the old woman curses as three girls help her up.

A man who has picked up the crutches hands them to her.

Tobe chuckles quietly. "Reminds me of my mother."

Daluchi drops her hands to her sides and pulls slightly away from him. She's never told him before, but she dislikes hearing him talk about his mother or brother. He craves something neither of them can offer—which she has more than enough of, but he seems to take that for granted—and it jars her the way a coconut grating machine does as its blades bump and rattle.

"My mother, God rest her soul. She never thought I could be happy. I wish she were still alive—"

"At least your father is still kicking," she cuts in.

He cups his chin thoughtfully. "I know," he continues. "I'm sure the old devil is looking forward to reuniting with her."

Daluchi almost scoffs when she pictures her own mother and father together again. Tobe takes the curtain's hem and rolls it between his thumb and forefinger. He says nothing but continues to feel the fabric, looking like he wants the floral patterns to rub off on his fingers. Something is nagging him. Something he wants to talk about, but he doesn't quite know how to go about it. Whatever it is, she can't figure it out.

*Has he finally come to his senses like the biblical prodigal son?*

"She was so full of bile the night she died. Not even my father who doted on her could make her happy," he begins.

At first, Daluchi thinks that he is musing aloud because his voice is low and flat. But then she realizes that he's sharing yet another pathetic story with her.

"She cursed me, cursed even my younger brother, who bought her presents every Mother's Day. She cursed the day she found out that she was pregnant with me. She never planned to have a child, let alone two boys. It was an accident, and my brother and I were a mistake."

Tobe's shoulders sag as he sighs.

"I sometimes wish she hadn't died from such misery, thinking that we never allowed her to enjoy her whole life. I wish that strange disease in her womb hadn't eaten her up. She gave me hell, true, she did, but I think no mother really hates her own flesh and blood. God knows that I always had something like that in mind—I mean, getting her a present. Something to show her that I couldn't hate anybody. I wasn't miserly with love. I gave her nothing, not even a Hollandaise wrapper. That's what I regret the most. Not having shown her that I was generous, my mother."

He reaches for her hand and grips it firmly.

His palm is clammy, and Daluchi is baffled that Tobe still pines for something that is beyond reach—his late mother and her love. She thought he would tell her what she herself had been pining to hear—a *different* confession that would lift her sour mood. She tries to make sense of his words, but she can't. First, it was about the *stupid* fish. Next, it was about his mother.

*Ogini bu nka?*

Daluchi stops herself from hissing. His recollection hasn't reassured her in any way. Here she is, concerned about what is alive and breathing, and he is busy garbling about what is past and dead. She doesn't understand why he tells her these things, what he meant about his being generous.

*Wasn't he the same person who told her on their first Christmas together that he hated sharing his toys with his brother when they were kids? That he enjoyed watching him cry after he seized his toys?*

A street vendor pushes his loaded cart blaring Wizkid's "Ojuelegba." Tobe lets go of her hand and starts humming the song. Daluchi shoots him an incredulous look and slowly shakes her head. Humming even harder, he flaps his arms and shimmies his chest to the music. He teases Daluchi, who, despite herself, manages to smile because he looks stupid.

"You know I can't wait to devour you, right?" Tobe lunges playfully at her, but she ducks out of his reach.

"I'm sure you will," she says before heading into the kitchen.

Daluchi bustles around there for a while. The dizziness seems to have eased. She scoops out some chicken pepper soup from the pot and into a china bowl, heaps some rice on a plate, wraps the cutlery in a napkin, and lays them neatly out on the tray.

At last, she appears in the living room, struggling a little with the tray because of her swaddled finger.

Tobe rubs his palms together. "Smells amazing!"

She sets the tray on the table. Her fingers still smell of chopped onion and garlic. Lifting her head, she holds his gaze for a few seconds.

*Is it possible that he hasn't loved me all this time, the two years we've been together?*

It hadn't taken much to love Tobe. He had seemed lost, in need of saving, that Sunday afternoon when she'd first met him at a pub while she preached to his fellow drinkers. She decided to save him and show him the right path. She scraped her little savings together from her clothing store and got him back on his feet.

Chewing, he says, "What would I do without you, Dally Baby?"

"You didn't pray."

Tobe slouches as he says grace. He then reaches a hand across the table. "Let me see. How did it happen?"

Daluchi winces a little under his touch. She thinks of her late father, a man with thin shoulders and small hands, who looked harmless but stung you with his jokes.

*Is this how my mother felt about him?*

"It doesn't hurt much, right?"

It hurts like love, she thinks and shakes her head. Her mother still seethes with thoughts of revenge, five years after her father suffered heart failure. Daluchi closes her eyes briefly to hold down her burning agony. No, the pain of a severed finger compares little to what she felt the day she found out Tobe was sleeping with another woman. For the last six months.

"Sorry. Sorry. Gently." He kisses the bandaged finger before he lets go of her hand. "But this is yum yum, dear." He sounds exuberant, like a little child, and smacks his lips. "Not even my mother can cook pepper soup like this. I like that it's peppery. The chicken is tender."

Tobe unbuckles his belt and strokes his belly. "You should do that cooking competition I told you about. And win the cash prize. How much is it again?"

Daluchi watches him slurp the remaining soup. Her spine tingles. He polishes off the last bit of chicken and belches into the air. She frowns at him and decides not to sew the tear on the couch.

"What?" He lifts an eyebrow and then lets out a chuckle. "*Maka Chukwu.* This is good, I mean, no, easily the best meal ever."

Her lips tilt open, but she says nothing. She can tell that he is grateful she cooks for him every night.

Tobe leans over and cups her cheeks with callused palms, pressing his lips against the spot between her eyes. He kisses it in a slow, feathery way, and she feels her temples quivering.

Her back arches.

Her breath flutters.

A lump rises in her throat.

Daluchi swallows and begins to feel tender, but she quickly hardens and pushes the lump back down. No, not now. Not tonight. She desires more, something more disarming than gratitude, something more abiding than his hairy body lying next to hers, his fingers drawing butterflies across her navel. She has already gone past the stage of sweet talk—of settling for less.

Daluchi looks at the empty soup bowl. She could nudge the table with her foot. The sound of china breaking into pieces might comfort her. She tries to remain calm, though she imagines a sharp piece cutting into her finger and manages not to wince. She sighs and tries to focus on the moment.

Yet an old image comes to mind. It is blurry, and then it gets sharper. She is thirteen years old but taller than most boys her age. Her classmates treat her as abnormal because of her height. Boys nickname her "Yokozuna" and "Mt. Kilimanjaro," but the girls call her "Tallie." Sometimes, at night, Daluchi sees herself growing taller and taller like the magical beanstalk in that children's story told in schools. Finally, she is so tall that her head punctures the roof, knocking it off completely. Everyone, including her parents, shrieks and flees in fright. Birds scatter in every direction, screeching at what she has become.

Daluchi shudders at this horrible image. She doesn't know why she remembers all this now or what it has to do with how she feels about Tobe. She clearly remembers jamming her foot into the crotch of one of the boys who often mocked her during break time. The boy had lain on the floor groaning, his hands tucked between his thighs, while their classmates laughed at him.

"Is there something you want to talk about, Dally Baby?" Tobe asks, reaching for the glass of water.

"No, not at all," she replies.

He sips some water, his eyes on her.

She wonders how she would react if he were to choke. Her mother wished that her father had choked to death. He had other children. Not one, but three—all from different women. They only found out at his funeral. The following day, her mother burned all his photographs but left his clothes. She regretted not having chopped off his penis while she had the chance.

Daluchi suddenly realizes that Tobe reminds her of her father: frail and funny.

"Agape's husband called me while I was on the bus."

"What happened? Did she lose her pregnancy?"

"No, nothing happened. Agape has given birth."

Daluchi touches her navel. "At last."

Tobe's younger sister was childless for over a decade. She married as a virgin but kept having one miscarriage after the other. In desperation, she visited doctors, priests, and spiritualists in different parts of the country. She searched for potions and portents in far-flung villages and bathed in rivers, including the Oguta Lake and Awhum waterfall, both rumoured to stimulate fertility in women. She chewed garlic and ginger, smeared her belly with all types of lotion, and even suffered strange fingers prodding her private parts. The only thing she probably escaped was having to lie naked under one of those strangers.

"Yes. At last." Tobe nods and peers at the painting of a rooster, a mother hen, and her chicks on the wall. He stares at it as if seeing it for the first time.

Daluchi had bought the colourful canvas print on a whim from a vendor at a makeshift motor park. The rooster is a splash of red, orange, and blue, while the hen is plain brown, and the chicks are all white.

He squinches his brow and looks away from the painting.

"We should see Agape tomorrow and take some of your pepper soup along."

"Is it a girl or a boy?"

"A chick," he says with a chuckle.

Daluchi swats him on the knee. "I'm serious."

"I wish it were a boy."

"Why?"

He clicks his tongue. "That might be the only child they ever make."

Something claws her belly, though Daluchi endures its sting. She remembers the catfish that he made her gut, its gooey eggs that curdled her stomach. Sometimes she dreams of having a child who looks like Tobe, but she doubts she could deal with two of him now.

She clears the table and returns the tray to the kitchen, still trying to hide the pain she feels in her finger. Dutiful, as always. Almost like her mother.

*Is this not reason enough for him to love me more than his lover?*

Back in the living room, Daluchi nestles in his arms while he reclines on the grey couch. He has eased himself out of his blue shirt and black chinos and is in a singlet and boxers. He burps out loud again and laughs softly, mischievously, to himself.

She clenches her jaw, ignoring him.

Tobe takes her hand and places it on his nipple.

She wants to squeeze it hard as if it were a blackhead, but instead she rolls her forefinger over it.

"So, tell me what happened to your finger."

"You just ate it. With the chicken."

He laughs again. "You always surprise me."

She laughs, too. "I cooked it for you."

"Goodness, you've finally learned to be funny."

"I'm serious."

Tobe stops laughing. "Yes, you always were."

He cranes his neck to look closely at her when she doesn't counter him.

Daluchi feels his body stiffen under her. The goosebumps on his skin graze her own arms. For a second, he is a statue. Then she feels his heart thump against her shoulder.

"Whatever this is, it isn't funny."

"Exactly."

Tobe seems to catch his breath. Then his nostrils flare. "Is that supposed to be a joke?"

"No," she replies, unblinking. "You ate my finger."

He jumps up, shoving her off him, but she steadies herself and slides back on the couch. He pulls away from her, his mouth twisting into a W. His eyes threaten to pop. He looks as though he is caught between pushing back a scream and losing himself to a retch.

Daluchi stares at him—his trembling lips, his hands fluttering toward his mouth—and almost smiles at his puckered face.

He speaks, but she can't make out his words, for they sound like a gurgle.

She extends a hand to him, crooking her fingers.

Tobe wobbles farther away from her, nearly bumping into the couch close to the door.

"No, you—you can't be—" he finally blurts. "I don't believe you."

"I know. Not everything is meant to be a joke," she says, dropping her hand on her lap. "See if she's willing to give a part of herself to you."

Daluchi calmly curls up on the cushions, picturing a fish with a man's head on it, its belly split wide open.

# THIS IS HOW I REMEMBER HER

**M**y cousins and I are side by side on the rug, fingers linked behind our heads. We just finished watching Jackie Chan and his funny karate kicks. They had laughed throughout the film, laughed like they were in a competition to see who could laugh the longest and hardest.

"Bube, what's wrong with your mom?" Olisa asks.

I pretend not to hear and scratch my knee.

The TV perches above our heads. A South African man with bloodshot eyes is rapping as if he is mad at everyone. I lift my chin to the picture of Mother Mary on the wall. She is staring down with blue eyes, her right palm on her flaming heart. If I lean close enough, maybe she'll tell me where my mom is. But she doesn't say a word.

"We heard some things," Olisa presses.

Their parents always speak about my mom in a whisper. They talk about her like she once used to be my mom but now belongs to somebody else. Like my *real* mom is no more, and someone new has been living inside her body. I don't know how long it's been since my mom and I have been separated, but whenever my uncle and his wife see me hanging around the living room or kitchen, they drop their voices and pelt me with smiles.

"Is it true?"

Ekeh jumps in just as his twin finishes speaking. "Remember Dad said not to ask him."

My cousins look at me as though I might sprout two more legs and a tail. They rarely stay quiet, buzzing like flies around my ears. They talk and talk like they have nothing else to do with their mouths. Even though I eat lots of eggs and butter here, I'd rather live with my mom.

I bite my nails. My cousins are thirteen, older than me by two years, and will be leaving next month for boarding school. I can't wait to have their whole room to myself. I will kick their pillows around. Their toys, too. Those dumb toy trucks you can bend this way and that.

*Transformers.*

The TV screen flickers with colourful images of P-Square. I like most of their songs because they make you jump and jiggle your shoulders. But right now, I hate how the brothers dance in this video, how they run their hands over the bodies of shiny girls in see-through clothing.

I look away and slip my mom's pendant out of my pocket.

"Do you always play with that?" asks Ekeh.

I stare at him and then continue rubbing the pendant—a small blue angel. My mom had suffered many miscarriages, so my dad bought it for her when I was born. He was happy he got a boy he could name after his father, one of the earliest catechists in our village back then.

"What happens if you lose it?"

I promised my mom that I never would. She hadn't known where my uncle was taking her, so she'd handed it to me, pressed it hard into my palm. She was sure that someone would steal it from her if I didn't hang on to it.

"I can't lose it," I say fiercely. "I won't."

Ekeh scoffs. "But what if you do?"

I peer at the pendant. If you hold it close to the light, the crystals will shimmer like a thousand blue stars. I shiver at the thought of losing the only thing I have left of my mom, the only thing that makes me believe she'll come back. I grip the pendant so tight that my nails dig into my palm, long enough that it starts to hurt a little.

My cousins draw away from me and begin whispering. I imagine they want to tease something out of me, so they can make a joke about my mom.

"People will laugh at you. *Ndi ojoo*. That's the world for you. Nobody but you can be strong for you," my mom had told me the afternoon she was taken away from me. She had sounded as though she was stumbling along a dim hallway and trying not to panic.

I'm not sure how long I've been staying here at my cousins' house. It feels like months, though it has probably only been days. It feels like I have done something wrong. Like I've been told to sit by myself in a corner, ahead of my punishment. There are times I want to sneak out of the house and go search for her, but I don't know where they are keeping her. It doesn't seem right that she has no family around her.

It's the way my mom wrapped her arms around me that I crave now. Whenever I had a nightmare, her arms rocked me gently back to sleep. In her arms, I could close my eyes and see my dad smiling at me. I think of how much I miss her, and I feel like I'm clawing out of someone else's body. A body too large and loose for me. A body that I'm continually being shoved back into.

My cousins stop whispering and turn to look at me. Their eyes widen. They stare at me like my arms have shrunken. I am panting, I realize. The sound of my breath frightens me. It's like a comb raking my dry skin. I decide to cut holes in their pillows once they leave for boarding school.

I jump to my feet and race out of the living room. But I trip over a throw pillow, smacking my jaw on the floor. The room crackles with laughter. My face stings as if it is covered in broken glass, and my ankle seethes. I pick myself up and, ignoring my cousins, limp out of the door.

Outside, the sun scalds the back of my neck. The gusty breeze stalks the nearby ube and guava trees, tugging at their leaves. The soothing scent of frangipani fills the humid air. I wonder if my mom had remembered to put her ointment in her bag, the one that reeked of mint, which she usually applied to my scraped knee or elbow.

Not long ago, she'd nearly made my heart burst out of my chest. My uncle and aunt had been talking about the military men that had gunned down some boys protesting on Douglas Road. I hadn't liked that my uncle sounded cheerful about the killings, so I left the living room and sat alone on the veranda. There was a half-moon, and I imagined the boys would have been chanting *Biafra* when the military appeared and sent them toppling over each other in a whiz of bullets. I was imagining their arms flailing and bodies squishing on top of each other when I sensed someone behind me.

I turned and almost flew off the veranda.

But a hand reached out, gripping me by the wrist. My mom called my name before I could scream. She held me so close that I felt as small as a butterfly. Her breaths, so quick, sounded confused and bore down on me. And I didn't feel as sure as I used to in her arms. I felt like I was trapped between two walls. Pinned under a musty blanket.

The air around me grew hot and dry.

I remember sneezing. I sneezed because my mom smelled like the washing left in a bucket overnight. She groaned as she crushed me against her body. She crushed me like she wasn't going to let go of me. Like she wouldn't see me for a long, long time.

*

My head feels so hot that I wonder whether I am not mixing things up. Sometimes I think I'm even imagining everything that is happening to me. It's like waking up in the middle of the night and finding yourself under your bed. Or like chewing your nails in a dream and waking up to see blood on your cuticles. And I don't like how my uncle and his wife keep moping at me anytime they run into me in the living room. As if I've slipped down a ditch, and they're wondering why I can't pull myself out of it. The angel pendant is the only thing that comforts me, that makes me feel everything will be all right.

My mom stopped mentioning my dad's name after he left home. She acted as though he never even lived with us, like he was an imaginary figure we both thought up. Like how I would lay out matchsticks to make a man. My dad was a matchstick man. He'd always come home late, and, sometimes, he never came home at all on weekends. When he was around, all he did was grumble and grumble about having to load goods on shelves at a warehouse. He grumbled about headaches and backaches. He hardly smiled and had no time for me, so I tried not to care much about him. What mattered to me was that I felt safe and warm anytime my mom enfolded me in her arms, even when she said the landlady would toss us out of the one-bedroom apartment.

I wonder where my dad is at this very moment. I doubt my mom knows where he is or whether he's living in another city. I try to picture him, but I can't. I remember catching my mom awake one midnight. She sat in bed, silent and still. I quivered, thinking she'd seen a ghost—my dad's. Around that time, I had stopped sleeping in the living room. I often lay on the floor next to my mom's bed. She hadn't noticed that I was up. I watched her gaze past the flickering lamplight in the room. She talked to herself once or twice. I pretended to be asleep when I saw her nod. I think she only began waking up at midnight after my dad disappeared.

Maybe she had never gone to bed at all.

My mom is strong and never complains. She didn't cry when my dad left or even when she lost her stall shortly after his departure. She no longer had any place to sell her yams because the governor wanted to put up buildings as tall as the Tower of Babel. Hundreds of women had gathered and protested the destruction. Some mothers scattered themselves in the dirt, while thugs dashed into the stalls and flung foodstuffs and goods everywhere. Bulldozers growled and tore down structures one by one. Shouts of sorrow knifed the air. That day, the women's voices formed a mighty chorus of tears. My mom had refused to join in.

She knows how to hold herself together, so I didn't think she would ever lose the firmness in her arms. I'd believed the rainbow in her face would last forever. I could have continued believing all this if my uncle and aunt hadn't shown up.

"Bube," said my aunt. "Your mom is not well."

"But we know a pastor," my uncle said, nodding to himself. "He is powerful. Very *powerful*." Small bags rimmed her eyes.

"He can handle her *case*." He said that last word as if my mom had become something to be folded up and filed away.

My aunt patted me on the shoulder. "For now, you'll live with your uncle. *Ighotara?*"

My uncle scratched his nose like he needed a pat himself. "Your mom will be well again. You'll see."

\*

There she stands, my mom, under the billboard of the governor's wife. The same woman whose husband destroyed her stall and those of other women. The woman has a bronze face flooded with a red-lipped smile. Chunky green, yellow, and purple beads decorate her neck. Across her chest, written in giant red letters, is:

WE TRANSFORM LIVES. CHANGE HAS COME.

I stare at my mom, just as onlookers also stare at her. She acts like she's about to climb on the broom and zoom straight into the clouds. Some shake their heads and whisper. Others lace their fingers atop their heads and sigh. They all act as though they fear that she's far beyond help.

My mom smiles. Not exactly at anyone, but at something above everyone's head. We are probably blurry to her. The smile I see on her face is different. I've never seen it before. I wish I never had.

My mom, tall, beautiful. She now looks like a twig in bits. Her shoulders are bony. When she smiles at something above us, I know that some worm, long trapped under the skin of her face, is eating its way through. That worm makes her grin strange, twisting her lips in a wormy way, like that film, *Alien,* my cousins and I watched some nights ago.

The crowd continues to swell. The women seem like they've had their ears pinched. It is the grin on my mom's face that does it. A shard of glass, it cuts into flesh.

My mom turns her back to them. Humming, she sweeps.

For a moment, I wish she is someone else's mom. She isn't mine. She sweeps so slow, so unhurried, like she has forever to sweep. She is half-covered in dust and looks worn, too, as though she now spends her nights sweeping shadows.

And the sun burns low, a squeeze of tangerine.

The air would feel nice, so nice, if it weren't for my mom.

I hear someone call my name.

I spin round. I can't make out whose voice it is.

A woman points at me. "That's him. Bube."

"*Le anya!*" says another. "Yes, that's her son."

Everyone drops their jaw at the sight of me. Their eyes are big and bulging. Their mouths roll faster than rotor blades. The crowd suddenly parts, and, in its middle, I stand like Moses without his staff. Countless eyes skitter all over my body, leaving me itchy. Their stares dig teeth into my heart.

My mom doesn't see me. It's as if she has old skin on her eyes, blocking her vision. I want her to turn around. I fix my gaze on her, willing her to look at me, but she's stuck in a world she will never exit, one that I can't enter.

It's like the strange ditch in my dream that threatens to swallow me each time I draw too close to its edge. I've been seeing my mom standing on the other side of that ditch every other week. Neither of us can get across it. It is so dark that I can tell that it has no bottom. I haven't been bold enough to bring myself to peer into its darkness either. Maybe it's because the ditch sometimes quakes at the very edge, as though it will crack and cave in fast if I dare move a foot closer. My mom can only yell at me to grab the thin, veined hand she is sticking out to me. Yet every time I stretch my body to reach for it, the ditch appears to widen a few inches more and heave toward my feet. I immediately pull back, sure that there's something alive but entrapped in its blackness. Though all of this happens in my dream, it somehow feels real once I wake up.

Now, I watch my mom sweeping dust and litter.

"Her son, you said?"

"Yes, poor boy."

"I hear he now lives with her eldest brother."

"Losing both parents at his age is so-o-o-o sad."

I can't close my eyes. I can't cover my ears either. Their voices buzz in my head like my cousins'. I imagine myself back in my uncle's home. Things replay themselves in slow motion, and I can hear my cousins telling me that my mom has fled the prayer house where she'd been sheltered. She has been found sweeping parts of Awaka where we lived before my dad left. I haven't yet sprinted out the door to go and find her.

I say to myself, I'm only dreaming.

"An ungrateful dog for sure," someone says too loudly. "*Onye iberibe.* Leaving his wife and son like that."

My mom pauses as if she heard what they called my dad. She turns around, gripping her broom. Her knuckles are jagged and white. Her cheeks are flaky like she's moulting. Her eyes creep over the crowd, then settle on me. Eyes, more moonless than I've ever seen, bore through me. She doesn't seem to recognize me. Maybe she has forgotten about me. Or maybe she is only pretending.

There was a man, a shell of a man, a wrinkled old man, who once sat at my school gate. He had shreds for clothes—that is, what was left of his faded army uniform. And he sang about the Biafra war, bony children with bellies the size of pumpkins, mothers with ribs dry as stalks. He sang about it almost every day, his voice a string of sighs, a slow-moving stream, a trace of something past and foul, grey with longing. Something had tricked his mind during the war, they said. That thing had snapped his mind apart shortly after. The look he gave us when we stopped to laugh at him. That was the same look in my mom's eyes now—eyes that had gone on a journey, far, far, into the night, and had forgotten their way home.

The air clenches, and I feel its jab below my heart. I blink back the tears, but my eyes hurt. I can see clearer now. I dip my hand into my pocket, squeeze the angel pendant, and bring it into the light. I want to hold out my palm to her, so she can see its glitter. She will see that it's still with me—safe, undamaged. And that I'm still here, waiting for her to come back.

My mom leaps forward.

The crowd scatters like flies off a half-eaten mango.

I remain standing, sure that she'll not hurt me, that she will, at last, recognize me.

She draws a circle in the sand with the broom, mumbling under her breath. Then she jumps into the circle and stands still for a moment, clutching the broom against her chest and squinting at all of us. She slowly raises her face to the evening sky.

"He's up there," my mom mutters, gripping the broom so hard the bones stick out in her knuckles.

Everyone throws their eyes up.

A few voices slither through the crowd.

"Who?" whispers a woman behind me.

"God?" another says.

"*Mba nu,*" someone else interjects. "She's probably referring to the governor's wife."

"Open the door. He's been waiting for me." My mom's voice quavers.

But that voice is not really hers. It sounds like water running through a sieve. Like the voice of the woman who used to speak to herself as she cantered up and down our neighbouring street. The woman had mysteriously disappeared after months of prowling the street, leaving behind her five children. Neighbours still talk about the pain her husband had burned into her when he ran off with her best friend.

"Mom," I whisper, afraid I might upset her if I speak too loudly.

"Waiting...waiting..."

I lift the pendant to my face, the crystals glittering. "Mom? Look."

She barrels out of the circle unexpectedly, and everyone scuttles backwards.

I keep still, the pendant tight in my grip.

She looks at me, her eyes lingering on the blue jewel. She doesn't say anything to me, though her face is wrinkled and pointed. Maybe she is trying to figure out what to say or how to say it. Or maybe she feels terrible that she hasn't been around for a long time now.

I match her gaze, longing for her to pull me into her arms. Like she always did whenever I felt unsure of myself, or scared, or cold.

*It's okay, mom,* I want to tell her. *Please, let's go home.* I would like her to know that it wasn't her fault that everything had gone wrong. I'd rather have her blame my dad than herself. But my heart is pounding hard, and the words refuse to come out of my mouth. The pounding causes my chest to hurt, so I can't even make a sound.

I've been holding my breath, but I let it out.

My mom appears to recognize me now, or so I imagine. Her face relaxes. She is opening her lips—

*My grip is loosening around the pendant*

and is about to speak.

*and my heart has stopped pounding.*

The toot of a bus horn a short distance away disturbs the moment.

My mom twists her neck to gaze around her as if to follow the sound. She frowns and releases a long hiss. For a minute or so, she makes no other sounds. She watches us while some people murmur in hushed tones amongst themselves. Suddenly, from her throat comes a sharp, frightful sound. She chuckles as she draws a slash across the circle with her broom.

And then she breaks into a run.

"Hah, this one she's running away," someone jokes. "Hope she doesn't end up in Ibadan."

"It's safer she ends up there than in a den of kidnappers or *ndi ogwu ego*," says another.

I don't want to be separated from my mom again. It is the ditch. I see it again—that strange ditch in my dream. I try again to grasp my mom's hand, but that ditch keeps widening and heaving. I move my eyes around me to check if anybody can see what's happening. No one notices anything. They are busy chattering in a dozen languages.

I long to leap over the ditch and run after my mom.

But my knees lock, my feet fail me. I can't even bring myself to scream for her to come back because my voice has folded into itself and refuses to rise.

The crowd is beginning to thin. One or two people could go after my mom. But nobody does. They pull away from me one by one, gnashing their teeth.

I bite down on the inside of my cheek, watching her blur into the shadows, wanting only to remember how she used to be tall, beautiful—her eyes of the moon. Not *this* her, unwashed for weeks, thin as if she has been living off grass. Not with that smile, so crooked and unlike any she's ever given me.

A smile that would remain with me until I was brave enough to accept that neither my dad nor my mom was ever coming back.

# NEIGHBOURS

There's something about my neighbour's face. I've been trying to figure it out since he, Mr. Kwento, moved into the apartment across from mine on the top floor, four months ago. The other two neighbours—a couple in their fifties and a single mother of two girls—live downstairs.

I hear Mr. Kwento's wife close their front door. I sneak to the window to steal a look at him. I flatten myself against the wall as he pops his head out of the car.

He calls out her name, his voice as gentle as a tap on the wrist.

"Anything?" his wife says from their balcony.

"My notepad on the cabinet."

I imagine him at his upholstered desk in his office—an exact man who organizes his life like clockwork.

She asks him if she should bring it down.

"Throw," he says.

I steal a peek as he catches the notepad and slides his car out of the gate.

\*

I know the hum of his Toyota Venza even while daydreaming. When I hear it in the late afternoon, I'm not sure if it's real or in my head. I heave myself off the couch and skulk to the window. Mr. Kwento turns off the engine, steps out of the car, and shuts the door. He carries a black laptop bag. He leans over to inspect

25

the hood and flicks at something I can't see from my window. I pull the curtain aside an inch more to see his face. As he straightens up, I duck down under the windowpane. I hold my breath, careful not to make any sound.

Before I can cross the living room, I hear a knock and freeze. At first, I think he is knocking on his own door. Then I realize he's knocking on mine. If I open the door, I'll be able to see his face up-close, but I'm rooted to the spot. He knocks once more, and my heart skips. I hear him ask if there is anybody home. He retraces his steps when his wife opens their door and welcomes him home.

*

I am drawing a caricature of Ben Enwonwu's *Christine*. The woman in the painting reminds me of my mother, who's been bedridden with a damaged kidney for five months or so. A sudden bang on my door jolts me, and I make a wrong stroke on the pointed chin. It's got to be Mr. Kwento. Has he caught me peeping through the window?

My stomach tightens.

I drop my pencil and brace myself for whatever will happen once I open the door.

"May I come in?" he asks when I turn the knob.

"Please." I give him a half-hearted nod.

Mr. Kwento sweeps his eyes across the living room as if he suspects someone is hiding behind the curtains.

I regard his lacquered face. There is not a single hair on it. It's like a baby's skin, so smooth I almost lean forward to run my fingers over it. He looks like a man who doesn't go a single day without pampering his face with powder. A man who inspects his face in his bathroom mirror every morning to see if a strand of hair has sprouted overnight. Or if any hairs have grown out of place. I can picture him smiling, satisfied with his appearance.

His hairless face reminds me that I haven't shaved my pubic hair for a long while. But this isn't what makes his face peculiar. There's something else about it.

I shut the door.

Mr. Kwento swaggers past me.

I bound to the couch and, plumping the cushions, I gesture for him to make himself comfortable. I pick up the empty can of energy drink and the half-eaten packet of digestive biscuits on the floor. I catch him eyeing my dishevelled living room.

"Sorry. I have nothing to offer—"

"I want you to do a portrait of me," he cuts me short, raising his hand.

I feel my stomach relaxing. So, he knows that I am an artist? We rarely run into each other, and he ignored me the few times I greeted him. Still, I'm excited about painting his face. Finally, I could find out why I'm attracted to it.

I fake disinterest in his request and tell him my fee is very high.

Mr. Kwento smiles as though he knows that I'm lying. "How much is high?"

"Eighty-thousand naira only," I reply. "But fifty-thousand naira for you because we are neighbours."

"How about thirty thousand this evening and the rest when you're done painting it?"

I might like him, after all. He is the kind of client I like doing business with—blunt and businesslike. A man who has no time to haggle over prices. I scratch my thigh, pretending to consider his offer. I wrestle with my excitement because I need the money to settle my mother's medical bills. Her kidney is in a mess, collapsing.

"I'm always paid in full."

"Fine, you'll get it this evening."

As I walk Mr. Kwento to the door, he stops midway and turns to face me.

"You were in yesterday evening, right?" His eyes hold mine.

I shake my head and immediately bolt the door behind him when he walks out.

*

Mr. Kwento doesn't come around that evening as he promised. Instead, he shows up on his way to work the next morning and hands me a wad of fifty thousand naira. It smells like him, full and fruity, its fragrance like a potpourri of crushed berries, nutmeg, and hibiscus—the kind of fragrance that greets your nose the moment you step into a florist's shop and makes you want to curl up on the nearest couch. I wonder if he sprayed perfume on the banknotes. It smells so nice.

"I'm a busy man." He smooths down his sapphire tie with his palm. He probably expects me to be in awe of his unsullied sense of style. He is a banker, so I suppose he's the type of man who embraces vanity with little effort.

There's a cute little crease in his chin, I notice.

"Let's start next week Sunday, okay? In my living room. I'll feel much more comfortable there than anywhere else."

I mull over his suggestion. It will take me five days to finish his portrait.

"Is there a problem?"

"No. I only paint from photos."

"I don't have to pose for you, do I? I mean, sit down while you draw?"

"No, a photo is enough," I tell him. "Any of your favourites would do."

"If you do a good job, I'll get you to do one for my wife as well. She's beautiful." Mr. Kwento pauses on 'beautiful,' I suppose to weigh my reaction. I keep a straight face, and he goes on. "She's my crown and glory."

*

I twist a pillow until the veins tighten in my hands. The canvas looms over me, blank, menacing. As if mocking me.

*His face. His face. His face.*

I'm afraid I might not get it right.

*

Two days later, Mr. Kwento drops by in the evening. He looks smart in his purple polo shirt and black combat shorts. Aside from his face, I have no problem with the rest of him. He is thirtyish, fit, and nimble—a proper model for sports wears. His skin reminds me of peanut butter, fair and smooth.

Hovering in the doorway, he asks, "Are these good?"

I study the three 5x7 matte photographs.

"Choose the one that you think best reflects..." He frowns and shakes his head. "My aura." He flicks a glance at his watch. "Let me know if any of those do not satisfy you. I have an entire album."

*

Mr. Kwento is photogenic, more handsome in photo than in flesh. His lashes are thick and long, unlike mine. I'm sure women would like to bump into him and have him catch them in his arms. He is smiling in all three photographs, but not all the way. His lips expose only a twinkle of teeth, and his eyelids crinkle only halfway—closer to a smirk than a smile.

Photograph #1: He is standing next to a mahogany desk, hands in his pockets, one leg crossed in front of the other. The desk is crammed with a laptop, files, a file rack, and a handset.

Photograph #2: An upper body shot. His arms are crossed.

The mahogany desk is behind him. To his left, the blue Venetian blinds brighten the background.

Photograph #3: He is sitting at the mahogany desk, his left elbow placed on its surface and his right arm slung over a part of the armchair. A grey steel cabinet towers behind him to the right.

None of the photographs are suitable. I could ask for the entire album, perhaps. I study them again and finally decide on the second photograph. In it, Mr. Kwento is gazing beyond the camera as if the photographer didn't exist at all. I like how he smiles in a way that doesn't slant his head or his eyes. He looks confident and powerful.

He is a man, who has nothing to hide.

*

The sun paints mauve, rose, and lemon in the horizon. The air smells chalky. Probably from the pastel stains under my fingernails. My cellphone buzzes in my pocket. I drift to the balcony and let my cellphone buzz until it stops. I suspect it's my mother; she is the only person who phones me twice in a row. I dread her calls and usually lose my appetite after speaking with her because she's afraid of her failing health. I also don't want to live in fear. I sometimes imagine that her kidney has worsened, and she must undergo surgery, which I can't afford. With the economy in a sewer, it's hard for many freelance artists to get by these days.

I watch some boys playing soccer in the street. They pause now and then to give way to oncoming cars, motorcycles, and tricycles. When they resume their game, a boy trips on the ball but manages to steady himself. His friends double over in laughter, calling him fake "Dinho" because he's sporting a Barcelona jersey with Ronaldinho embossed in yellow on the back. The barbershop across the road starts blasting Yemi

Alade's "Johnny." Some girls, lounging on the deck of a nearby pub, hoot with delight and spring onto the sidewalk. They break into an electric dance, jerking their hips and limbs.

I wonder what it'd feel like to throw myself down from the balcony. How would I land? Would there be pain? About four or five years ago, a baby in another building had slipped through the rails of a balcony and landed on its bottom. When people gathered to pick it up, it was screaming so shrilly that veins bulged along its throat. There were no bruises on its body, only steaming yellow poo streamed down its legs.

I sense someone is watching me. I turn and see my neighbour's wife hovering on their balcony. She stares at me with all the veins in her eyes. I raise my hand to wave at her, but her gaze flies over my shoulder, past me, just like her husband's had in the photograph.

*

"Who's there?" I grunt.

I already know it's him. Mr. Kwento has popped by twice this week.

"Me, neighbour," he replies, as expected.

When I wrench the door open, he shrinks back into the hallway, like he has stumbled upon a millipede reared on two legs. The thicket of hairs on my lizard-lean chest—as untamed as my dreads—must have alarmed him. I'm dressed only in cut-off jeans. My room is hot and stuffy. The fan is creaky and annoying, and the heat from the past few days could roast an egg left outside on the asphalt. So, at night, I sleep naked on the rug, half swimming in a pool of my sweat.

"Come in," I say.

Mr. Kwento lobs an excess of smiles at me, walks in, and sits down. He doesn't seem as watchful as usual. I sit cross-legged on the floor.

"You have a musical voice, Golibe," he says. "Deep, tender."

This is the first time he has called me by my name. It feels terrific. Before now, he has made no eye contact with me and strode fast every time I tried to greet him. I cross my arms when I catch his eyes roving away from my nipples. When I was in secondary school, I reported some boys who liked to fondle each other's breasts to the principal. I drop my arms now and wonder what Mr. Kwento's childhood was like—if he, too, went to an all-boys boarding school. Was he fondled as well?

He runs a hand over the cushions. I follow the trace his fingers make on the fabric. He appears hesitant, as if the sight of my body has changed something between us. I'm tempted to ask him if he'd like to touch my chest.

"Been meaning to tell you." Mr. Kwento sounds husky. "Your voice is lovely."

He is not his usual self today, I suspect. Something is bothering him. He's hurting. I feel like gripping his hand to comfort him. I sense that he wants to say something about his wife—something he hasn't yet told anyone. Perhaps the real reason she hardly leaves their apartment. I can count on one hand the number of times I have seen her outside the gate.

"Tell me where it hurts," I whisper.

Mr. Kwento leans sideways and stares at me. "What does that mean?"

"It's a song. Milli Vanilli. From their album, *The Moment of Truth*."

"Oh." He nods twice. "Have you ever thought of becoming a musician? Not the kind of crap Timaya and his ilk are spitting out into the airwaves. Something much more artistic. There's plenty of money in it, you know."

I scoff and shake my head.

"I've noticed you don't keep friends. Is it because of the clothes you wear?"

I remain silent. I don't care if he meant it as an insult because I know he is in pain.

Mr. Kwento stands up and says rather briskly, "Anyway, you have a portrait to finish. I have a wife to take care of."

*

Just when I think I'm asleep, I hear a crash and scramble out of bed. It takes a few seconds for my eyes to adjust to the darkness in the room, but I recognize the angry voice in the other apartment. Mr. Kwento is swearing to himself. I wonder what happened to him. Maybe he has banged his shin against the table. He could still be hurting from whatever he wanted to talk to me about.

*

"Hey, how's it going?" he asks cheerily, studying a painting hanging on the wall.

Onobrakpeya's *Have You Heard* and Okeke's *Fortune Pot* hang next to Picasso's *Les Demoiselles d'Avignon* and Grillo's *Snake Charmer* above my couch. On both sides of the living room door are Van Gogh's *Self Portrait* and Nwoko's *Beggars*. I like to create caricatures of masterpieces for the thrill.

"You did all these?"

I yawn in reply, hoping he understands that he should leave. Painting his face has left me feeling depleted. My spine aches. The bone in the back of my neck is sore. I feel like I've torn a muscle from too many hours spent standing and sitting. I fret about getting his face right.

"You're talented." Mr. Kwento points at a parody of the *Mona Lisa.* "But *that* is ugly."

I stifle another yawn then bite my lip so as not to snap at him. He continues to admire the other paintings: landscapes, still lifes, and self-portraits.

"Golibe, I envy you. There are times I wish I'd waited a few more years."

I stare at him, wanting, for some strange reason, to dunk my head in a bathtub of iced water.

"Not that I'm bored with being married, no. Well, you've seen her yourself, my wife. Have you? I love that Machie is fleshy. I can't stand skinny girls. No boobs, no butt, I might as well be touching myself." His chuckle is cautious, shaky. "Can you be trusted with a secret?"

I'm curious. I lean forward, catching a whiff of my unwashed armpits—the bitter smell of grease. There was a time I used to scratch my armpit and bring my fingers to my nose and take a sniff. I'd found the scent itself soothing.

"Never mind." Mr. Kwento shakes his head as though realizing himself. He steers himself toward the door. "I am expecting a striking portrait of myself."

*

My mother wheezes as she speaks, or so it sounds to me. Breathing has become a strain for her. In my head, she is climbing a hill. While she complains about her health on the cellphone, all I can think about is money, money, money. Maybe I should rob the bank at the corner of FRSC junction. Usually, there are only two armed policemen at the security booth. I wonder what it would feel like to get shot.

American films sometimes make it feel glorious in a weird way—a man staggers backwards in slow motion, his hands clutching his bleeding chest, his eyes gleaming with astonishment, his mouth hanging open like a revelation. Then a sliver of memory or light unfurls before him. Some men see an angel before their sight finally dims.

"It's like a baby's poo, the food the nurses serve us there."

I snap out of my thoughts and put the cellphone on speaker.

I pace around the room; her wheezing still burns my ears. My mother rambles on about the nurses, how they slap stubborn patients on the thigh and chide the clumsy ones for behaving like babies. At one point, she yelled at a nurse and nearly pulled her ear to set her head straight. I'm tempted to ask her whether she remembers that her late husband had a quick temper and a quick hand. He used to slap the stars and lightning out of my head anytime I did something wrong.

"Prison wardens, that's what I call those nurses."

I linger at the window, and the sun's glare hits me smack between my eyes. I grimace and turn away from the window.

"Golibe, you are not saying anything."

Mama, go straight to the point, I want to say, but I say out loud, "What do you want me to say?"

"I can't hear you well. Are you nursing a cold or what?"

I massage my temples, carefully weighing my response.

"Can you speak up, my son?" Her voice rises sharply.

"You know I'm working." I grunt and sink into the couch with a thud.

"Prrrr. That kind of work." Her wheeze sounds precisely like a snigger. "Why not get a proper job that pays well? I want you to stop by at the hospital and bring me some proper food."

I clench my teeth and stop myself from snapping at her. She's becoming more demanding by the day, and her illness is unscrewing a few nuts in my brain. If she continues like this, I'll not be surprised if I wake up one morning and stroll around the front yard, naked.

"Mama, you know I don't like cooking," I reply as calmly as possible. "Except when you want some noodles."

"Golibe, I keep hoping you'd someday get a proper woman to—"

"*Biko nu*, Mama. Let's not go there. Please."

She clicks her tongue. "The way you're sounding. I hope everything is okay with you. Are you eating well?"

"I'm fine." I repeat those words three times, like a mantra. To remind myself that it's useless to get more worked up than I already am.

"I hope you *really* are."

"You never once stood up for me, Mama."

"Stood up for you? What do you mean?"

"Those times Papa slapped and kicked me."

A sudden gulp of air in the background. Her breathing is loud, more laboured than usual. I've hit her where it hurts. My mother never tried to stop my father from beating me. Instead, she disappeared from the house and only reappeared when he'd finished hitting me. Even after he passed away, she and I never spoke about his violence. Silence seemed the safest place to hide in—for me, at least. And probably for her, too. Maybe we couldn't find a common language to decry his violence then. Or maybe we were too afraid to mention it at all.

There's a long pause between us before she finally responds in a wobbly voice: "But you know your father, I couldn't contain him." She breaks off to catch her breath. "He never stopped getting angry. He couldn't deal with..." She pauses again for a moment. "But Golibe, why are you bringing this up now?"

"Something you said about the nurses," I explain.

My father must have left a gash in her heart, even though he died over a decade ago. It's strange that I hardly think much about him. He had grown angrier shortly after the burial of his only sister. She and some women had been trekking to their kindred farm when a gang of herdsmen had waylaid and raped them. Relatives later found the women's bodies mutilated under a pile of palm fronds. When the village elders visited the police and realized that they had no interest in arresting any herdsmen or pursuing the case, my father had taken his anger out on me.

My mother is quiet, though her wheezing fills the air in my room. Did she ever think of leaving him and hiding someplace?

Or was she too terrified that he'd find her eventually and deal with her? I long to ask her, but I suspect that I might hurt her some more.

I sink deeper into the couch. I rest my head on the cushion and let out a long sigh.

"I will send you the money." I squeeze my eyes shut.

"*Chukwu gozie gi.*" She bursts into a round of prayer before I can hang up.

*

My scalp tingles at the sound of the knock on my door. I stomp across the floor, eager to see the flustered look on my neighbour's face when I yank the door open and tell him to *fuck off!* I snatch my hand from the doorknob the instant I hear an unfamiliar voice. It is not Mr. Kwento as I expected, but his wife.

Machie calls out again, urgent, but cautious.

It's rare to see her outside their apartment. So what could she possibly want from me?

She nearly stumbles into me when I pull the door open.

"May I take five minutes of your time?" She pants.

I long to say, *No! No! No!* and shake my head so strongly that my dreads would fly and crackle at her. But she blinks her big round caramel eyes at me, and the words fail me. Although her husband's eyes trouble me, I am smitten by hers. She has a way of staring at you as if she's unsure whether to smile or not.

I gesture to the couch.

Machie secures herself between two of the cushions. There are empty packets of cookies and squashed cans scattered on the floor. My dirty shorts and shirts spill in a tangle out of the closet. I expect her to wrinkle her nose at it all—even at the codfish smell in the air. But she does not squirm. She doesn't move at all.

"He has been visiting you." Machie sounds reproachful.

I turn down the volume on the radio as TuFace's song about one love fades away. Sitting across from her, I mutter, "Who?"

"Jarvis."

"Who is Jarvis?"

"My husband."

"Oh, is that his name?"

Machie doesn't answer.

"I'm doing his portrait."

"That's why I'm here. Stop. I want you to stop."

"Why?" She's beginning to get me confused.

She clasps her fingers on her lap and lowers her head for some seconds. An air of heaviness wafts around her, and she appears to be wrestling with it. I watch her shoulders heave and drop. Her neck is long—I want to rest the back of my hand on it. I'd like to draw her neck. It's the kind that stands out in a portrait.

"To spite me. He is doing it to spite me."

I almost chuckle. "Are you joking?"

Machie casts a glance around my living room. There is something shifty, frantic, about her now. Like a rat sneaking out of its hole to carry out some mischief on the half-eaten bread on the small table in the room. Before long, her words flow out, running like water down the stairs, all over the place.

"It's like I'm trapped in a museum from another world. I'm frightened. Our bedroom is full of his photos. There is one of us both on the bathroom door. I hate how he's smiling in that photo, like he knows I'm helpless. I don't love him like I did before; that's if I ever did. He thinks that by putting all his photos everywhere, then I won't have any choice but to love him again. And soon, he will have that horrible portrait hanging in our living room. I'll be forced to see his face anywhere I look in our apartment. He's sure I'll be reminded of how I can't live without him."

After she finishes speaking, she seems so shaken that she must feel like I'll be giving her a heart attack if I hand over the finished portrait to her husband. When I don't respond, she wavers on the edge of the couch, seeming desperate.

"I'll double whatever he paid you."

This could be a jackpot!

But is she in her right mind? I doubt she knows what she's saying. I don't know what to say myself. I once read something about people who avoided contact with friends. Is that what she's dealing with? Is that why she usually peers down the balcony?

The realization causes a chill in my bones.

*Eyaaa,* this is what has been troubling Mr. Kwento! No. I can never relate with someone who is losing it. Besides, I have enough troubles of my own. My mother's kidney problem. My lack of sleep. The wooziness I feel each time I linger too long on the balcony.

Standing up, I point to the door.

"You should leave now."

Machie straightens her shoulders. "God knows I have tried, but I can't stand his face anymore."

Her words stagger me. My body shudders, and I feel bubbly inside. There it is—she can no longer stand his face. Nothing is wrong with me. I'd thought I was losing my mind over nothing. Like I was obsessing about nonsense. I've been worried the whole time, but she has confirmed it now. There is something about his smooth, baby face. Something I still haven't figured out.

Machie's eyes glow. Her expression has changed, for she looks somewhat animated, like I've mysteriously given her a reason to believe in something. She must have seen my expression change too.

"There are things I could tell you about him, but you'll never believe me. I wouldn't wish for any woman, even if she were desperate enough, to marry his kind of person."

"I'd like to help, um, but I can't." I do not tell her that I'm also desperate. That I desperately need the money.

"You may have noticed that I'm always at home. He doesn't let me work. He insists that other men are not to be trusted. He doesn't want other men staring at me." Machie pauses and tugs at her puffy blouse. "He knows my bra size, can you imagine? He has the password to my email account, checks the messages on my phone at times. Did I get a university degree to become a full-time housewife? He tries hard to make me feel loved. He tries too damn hard. It feels like my chest is locking up. Where is the space to be myself? What is love if you can't breathe?"

Her face twitches. I can tell she hasn't been sleeping well either.

"Tell your closest friends," I suggest. "Let them help you sort out whatever issues you both have."

Machie sneers at me like I've just blurted out the stupidest thing. "You don't get it, do you? He won't let me have friends. He hardly invites anyone over. He thinks his friends are envious of him. He is afraid of women, but he doesn't admit it. He's worried that if he gives me even a little space of my own, I might become like his mother."

"What about your brother? Or your sister? Your mother?"

"My mother is the last person I could tell."

"Why?"

"She never trusted him. His face is too full of smiles, she always said, too smooth, too neat. A man in love with himself. I didn't see what she saw. I was in love with the surface, his good looks, the way he spends money. He is the kind of man girls long for. But I see it all now."

*Leave him*, I want to tell her. *Leave him with all his handsomeness.* I don't want to sound stupid again, so I say instead, "Neighbour, you can work it out with him. Trust me."

Machie shakes her head fiercely, and I understand that my attempt not to sound stupid failed. I now understand why she has been teetering on the balcony.

"I am not his mother." The words jet out of her mouth as she rises from the couch. "I'll never be like her."

And she bangs the door shut on her way out.

\*

"Bro, this face looks familiar." Mr. Kwento refers to the drawing of his wife lying on the centre table. He has stopped calling me Golibe. Maybe he thinks his portrait might bring us closer than just neighbours.

After his wife left my apartment yesterday afternoon, I couldn't focus and continue his portrait. To my dismay, I painted a confusing swirl of strokes. I didn't think he would recognize the smudged face, his wife's neck.

"Did my wife come here?"

I frown. "Why would you ask that?"

Mr. Kwento smiles. "She may be curious to find out how far you've come with the portrait."

"I can't do a good job if you keep interrupting my process. Don't blame me if I fail to create something *striking*."

"Bro, are you trying to say you want me to stop dropping in?" Disbelief rumples his face. "I've been enjoying our chats." Then he says, "It's been over a week. When should I expect my portrait?"

"Friday. Before Friday."

He whoops like a teenager. "I'm most eager to see my wife's reaction."

I remember the sound of something crashing in their apartment some nights ago. I almost ask him if he had a fight with her. Or had she been smashing some of his photos?

"She'll be impressed," I say. "You have a unique face."

He stops gushing. A shadow crosses his features as he strokes his chin with the back of his hand. "You don't know Machie. She prefers being on her own. She has this...um, no.

How should I put it? Well, what makes you think she will be impressed?"

My stomach churns. I think of my mother and father.

I only reply, "Every woman loves her man."

Mr. Kwento grins. "I find you to be an interesting person, I mean, bro. Friday, huh? You'll bring my portrait to my living room. I shall have a bottle of whisky on hand. Oh, I have this special Australian Shiraz. I also have the pinotage my boss gave me when he returned from South Africa. I'm a wine expert, mind you. A collector, too. You drink, right?'

"I have a light head," I say, not liking the idea of staying for long in a room with him and his wife.

Mr. Kwento breaks into a soft-bellied chuckle. "A light head?" he says as if savouring the phrase on his tongue. "Anyone who sees you for the first time will think you are a chain-smoker. I don't mean to insult you, bro. Faces and appearances, do you get the picture I'm painting?'

His remarks sting, but I smile out of a quaint sense of politeness.

"I'd better go now. But you'll be getting drunk with me." He touches my arm before walking out of the living room.

*

Sitting on my rocking chair, I peer through the rails of the balcony. The sky is rolling out its sheaves of orange and lavender and transitioning into grey patches. I can see a star or two if I squint. There is a power cut in the neighbourhood. Generators grumble here and there, and lights flicker in the windows of adjacent buildings. Across the street, a mother yells for her daughter, threatening to use a pestle on her. In the distance, the late evening traffic hums along. It's like the hum of waves ebbing on the shore. I close my eyes, and the hum fills my ears.

A bloodcurdling cry snaps me out of my reverie. A dog is yelping in pain as if its foreleg is mangled. I almost get up and lean over the balcony to look at the injured creature, but I don't because the acrid tang of burned meat wafts from the street below, tainting the air. The last time I ate suya was with my mother. I sip my usual energy drink, wishing I had given her more money.

*

I hear a bang and scurry out of my bed. Someone has crept into my living room. I reach for my cellphone on the floor. My heart begins to drum. Gun-toting men visited our neighbour-hood sometime in the past, and somehow only our building and a few others hadn't been robbed. One of those men had shot a tenant who foolishly attempted to confront them. Fortunately for the man, he was shot in the mouth.

"Who's there?" I whisper, turning the flashlight on and sweeping it around the room.

There is no one in my room. I'm about to heave a sigh of relief when someone slams a door shut. I flinch. Another sound is coming from my neighbour's apartment. I slink across the room, the light cutting a tiny white path through the darkness. I unlock my front door and tiptoe out. Holding my breath, I place my ear against my neighbour's door.

Someone is sobbing from inside.

*

The next day Mr. Kwento comes around and sits on my couch. Until I finish painting his portrait, he is going to be a leech. He leaps up at once, grabbing at his behind. He turns around and glares at the couch as if it is covered in shards. He sat on an empty can. I watch him flick the can. It clatters across the floor. He positions himself carefully on the couch again.

"I used to gulp those energy drinks like an addiction," he murmurs like he still has a craving for them. "Not anymore, though. You see, Machie and I are trying again to make a baby, after her third miscarriage. Only five years in marriage, and she believes it has something to do with our blood type. We're incompatible, she thinks. She has these odd ideas, but I love her still." He stops talking. "I'm not interrupting you, am I?"

Lauryn Hill sings on the radio, her low, soulful voice uncoiling my stiff muscles.

"Would you like something to drink?" I ask, watching him closely as if his flaws are sharpening.

Mr. Kwento scratches the back of his neck, looking more stressed than worn. He frowns at the radio as if its presence will worsen his mood. "That's kind of you. But no, bro, thank you."

"You sure you don't want anything?"

"Maybe a smoke. Something to smoke. Do you have a cigarette?"

Was he serious? I reply, "I don't smoke."

He rubs his knees with both hands like he's anxious. "But I do. I never smoke at home. Machie doesn't know. She might suspect and say nothing about it." His voice is tense, faltering.

I lean toward the radio and turn it off, ending the soulful voice.

"Don't." He sounds too firm, almost bossy.

I straighten and stare at his raised hand. His wedding band glistens.

"Turn it back on," Mr. Kwento says, dropping his hand to the cushion. "I like that song."

I ignore his tone, though I am surprised that he listens to hip hop. He strikes me as a classical music fan or somebody who listens to some monotonous water sounds. I flick the radio dial, and Lauryn Hill returns.

He sings along to the lyrics of "The Miseducation of Lauryn Hill," swaying gently back and forth. His eyes are closed. His hands are tented over his belly.

I sit down and try not to smile. He tries too hard to make me feel loved, his wife had complained. Was she taking contraceptives in secret?

Mr. Kwento stops singing, opens his eyes, and gives me a flickering smile. "Do you know I provide her with everything any man of my status can offer, yet she is not happy?" he says.

"Are you talking about…?"

"My wife, yes, of course."

"Okay."

"Bro, I loved my dad, but I don't want to be like him. He's late, but let me give you a picture of the kind of man he was. He spoke very little, avoided quarrels with anyone, and liked to smile a lot. Aww, that smile riled me up. He couldn't even bark to save his skin. My mom monopolized the conversation whenever relatives and friends dropped by our house. On the other hand, my dad would sit on his chair listening to them, at times bobbing and nodding, smiling and chipping in words like a little bird. He was a world-class architect, revered by his peers—but you know what? You can have all the degrees and titles, bro, but any woman can still make a nincompoop out of you. Think of Samson. Think of Solomon. Let's not talk about David. Or past African dictators. You can see that my mom is a lioness—no man or woman born on earth could cow her. My dad was too tame for my liking, so she took advantage of him. That's how it is with women. Give them a single inch, and they take a yard or two before you can say, *hey, hold on!*"

I think about my father and couldn't recall any time he was ever tame. I would rather have a lapdog father than a brute any day.

Mr. Kwento continues speaking as I get up to fetch myself a glass of water at the kitchen sink.

"You must be careful around women lest they pat you on their lap—that was my dad's fate. I don't know whether to feel sad for him or not. It is all in the past, in any case. Still, to even think of what he had to go through at the hands of my mom. Every man must stamp his authority at home unless he wants his woman to transform him into her lapdog. My dad, for all his education and accolades abroad, had a high schoolteacher rule him. He finally died from heart complications. Women will outlive their men. Is it any surprise that many of us die miserably in the end? But don't get me wrong, my mom loved my dad so dearly that she was ready to tear anyone into pieces if they raised their voice at him back then. Such love, and yet she lorded it over him. She had him under her armpit all the time, but I've told her to stay out of my marriage. I can't have her tell me how to run my home or turn Machie against me."

Mr. Kwento stops speaking and begins pulling at his eyelid. He plucks a hair, inspects it, and flicks it to his feet. Then he rubs his thumb and index finger.

"That's where I'm coming from, you understand, bro? I believe every married woman should dress for her husband, not wiggle her hips and boobs everywhere in the name of fashion." He stutters only briefly. "Like she is trying to catch the eyes of other men. Bro, you see, I work hard for my money, and I can't have any woman telling me about her space and rights. Machie is nothing without me. She refuses to see that." He arches an eyebrow at me. "I don't think I have seen anyone coming to visit with you."

"By anyone, you mean?" I twirl a strand of my dreads between my fingers. I feel he has been spying on me the same way I've been peeping at him.

"I want to trust you," he says, stifling a yawn. "But you don't talk much. People who talk little can be, you see, like, I mean, unpredictable."

I hold his gaze, sure that Mr. Kwento is gauging my reaction. Though he looks exhausted, his eyes remain probing. Maybe he also hasn't been sleeping well.

"You see what I mean? Another person would have blown up, but you took my words so coolly like they didn't even matter."

"I'm an artist," I say, almost adding, *not a boxer*.

Mr. Kwento jerks his head at an angle and studies my expression. He might have misread my reply. Then he laughs, more to himself than at me. "So, what do you do for fun?"

"Are you asking if I have a girlfriend?" Perhaps he finds me appealing in a weird way.

His cheeks flush. "Uh—no, no. I don't mean it like that." He shakes his head, looking suddenly embarrassed. He looks cute, despite his obvious discomfort.

I let a smile tease a corner of my mouth. "I used to have a houseplant," I say. "Can't remember its name, but I think it's one of those plants that drink plenty of water. I talked to it and cared for it." I point to a cluttered bamboo rack by the window. "The vase used to sit there, facing the sun. I liked to watch the tips of the leaves catch the light. There were times the leaves looked so green that they glistened. I don't want to look back too much, but I remember one day I saw that I had snipped a leaf while shutting the window. I picked up the leaf. I couldn't draw a single line throughout that day. It was as if I had snipped a bit of my skin. No, it was much worse actually, like the blunt edge of a couch had snagged my toenail."

I close my eyes a moment, the memory a little unclear.

I continue speaking, "I never knew one could feel that way, but I soon realized anybody could get attached to things that weren't human. I realized that fact, surprisingly, right at that moment. It was a moment of clarity, your eyes open to the dawn. But also of loss, your heart shrinks from the chill. It's like going to bed feeling you're happy, only to wake up the next day not knowing why you'd felt happy. Or you now realize that you've been lonely and sad all the time, without knowing why you're even sad. I don't know if I'm making much sense. After a while, or maybe days, I came back to myself and made peace with the plant. I got busy with my stuff, drawing, painting, the whole canvas. Then, one morning, as I pulled the curtains aside, the blue of the sky caught my eye, the kind of blue you probably see hours after it has rained in the morning. Then, you see, I saw that my plant's leaves had turned brown. The soil in the vase was dry as paper because I had forgotten to water the plant. It might have been weeks. A month. I don't want to dwell much on what's gone now, but the poor thing. It didn't deserve to die like that. Imagine dying of thirst. I can't tell you how my body felt at the time."

I sigh and give him a full smile.

Mr. Kwento knits his brow and lets his gaze linger briefly on the rack.

I continue after a pause. "A friend of mine, well, he's not my friend anymore, you see, because he died in a car crash along Ninth Mile highway. Anyway, he had a different experience with his own pet. He travelled out of town for a week. While enjoying himself in Lagos, he recollected that he hadn't put out enough feed for his caged bird. Imagine having to starve to death. What I mean to say is, some of us have no passion for relationships."

Mr. Kwento says nothing. Whether my stories have stunned or offended him, I can't tell. I know that we haven't spoken this much before, in each other's presence, so he could be surprised. Meanwhile, the living room smells of acrylic, wax, and glue—acrid in a sweet, heady way. I inhale, recollecting my days at the art college when I used to smoke marijuana.

"People die. People die like flies every day," he finally says, stroking his jaw in a slow, brooding way. "So, what's the big deal? Don't we all eat chicken? Are they not birds too? We slaughter cows and make suya from them—who cares?"

His bluntness stuns me. Where did that come from?

He holds my gaze without batting an eyelid. I begin to feel uneasy because I can perceive that something he has long bottled up is chewing him from the inside. Something bitter and jagged.

He has been sitting upright the whole time; now, he leans back on the couch, hands on his thighs, legs crossed at the ankles, carelessly exposing a glimpse of his broad tan chest. The first two buttons on his plaid short-sleeved shirt are open at the throat, and the bloom of dark curly hairs on his chest grips me. He clears his throat, and I quickly move my gaze to his white sneakers.

Rihanna is crooning on the radio about the monster under her bed.

I want Mr. Kwento to leave my apartment and never return until I'm ready to hand him his portrait, but I don't know how to tell him or how he would react. He appears visibly upset. It must have something to do with my plant and the dead bird. When I raise my head, I catch him watching me. He has uncrossed his legs and is kneading his toes deep into the carpet. His face darkens as he prods the fabric, probably wanting to remove an invisible stain only he can see.

"Turn that thing off!" He points at the radio.

I feel the shock of ice on my back and recoil. I can't believe he just snapped at me in my own apartment. He must have noticed my shock because he drops his hand on the couch and apologizes.

"I'm sorry. I'm sorry." He twists a part of the cushion. "I don't know what got into me. I haven't been feeling well these days. I, um…never mind. Machie loves that song, and I don't."

Mr. Kwento rises from the couch and tugs his shirt down over his black jeans. In a blink of an eye, a bright smile surfaces on his face, masking his irritation.

I maintain my cool.

"She must have finished preparing dinner by now."

"To love is to lose," I tell him. "Take care."

Mr. Kwento spins round and stares at me with his mouth open, as if to say, *So, you know a thing about love, after all.*

*

I see Machie hugging her elbows on the landing. She looks jumpy, even in her white ruffle blouse. The dress must be expensive, but it gives her a starchy appearance—that of a village headmistress. I walk past her, having made it clear that I don't get involved in people's mess.

"I saw you coming in." She speaks in a cheery tone that sounds false to me.

It is too late. The portrait is finished. Did it ever occur to her that I could have told her husband that she had tried to discourage me from finishing his portrait?

Machie smiles at me without looking hurt by my silence. As I glance away from her face, I imagine her diving from the balcony, her arms outstretched, her white dress billowing like wings. The idea for another painting comes to me at that moment.

"What's that?" She points at the black plastic bag in my hand. "Paint?"

"Lunch," I mumble.

To my bewilderment, Machie suddenly lashes out and clasps my wrist. I flinch at the coldness of her fingers. She leans too close to me. Her breaths, tinged with cinnamon, tickle my ear.

"Do you understand women?"

Her question throws me like a shove. I swallow and try not to imagine her naked. If I could just touch her neck. I switch the bag to my other hand and pull away from her.

"I don't keep women if that's what you mean."

Machie glances down as though she can't imagine how I deal with my urges.

"Come," she whispers, grabbing my hand again and pulling me along to their apartment. "I only want to show you something."

*

I am back in my studio, my mind spinning. I knead the back of my neck. Sometimes, when I can't focus on my art, I start to doubt myself. Having seen several photos of Mr. Kwento splashed everywhere in their bedroom, I swear I will never take my sanity for granted. A moment ago, it had felt to me like I'd entered a shrine—their bedroom, only that it had stylish furnishings, heavy teal curtains, and was awash in warm terracotta tones. Its aura had been surreal and just as staggering.

"Who is it?" I bark when I hear two quick taps on my door.

Machie starts to say, "You left your lunch..." the moment I fling the door open.

I snatch the bag from her hand and thump the door in her face before she can finish her sentence. I toss the bag across the floor, cursing the devil for inviting her and her husband into my life. I turn around and gasp in surprise as I spot the spilled contents of the bag on the floor.

A wedge of banknotes. It's more than fifty thousand naira.

I imagine the joy in my mother's voice.

*

On the balcony, I think of my dead houseplant. My dead friend and his dead bird. Sometimes we kill by accident. We kill what we love by accident. My father's face suddenly crosses my mind. A policeman had shot him twice in the chest because he'd refused to stop his danfo bus promptly when they flagged him down at their checkpoint. His passengers had instantly bolted out of the bus and into the surrounding bush, leaving him behind to bleed to death. Fire exchange with armed robbers, that was how the police reported it.

I sigh and hold out the painting under the eye of the moon. What I have created takes hold of me and leaves my knees tingling. My fingers itch.

Perhaps I should keep this portrait to myself.

*

I watch Mr. Kwento study the portrait he has been expecting for the last three weeks. He is struggling to decide what to do with it. He looks swollen, unable to hold the little storm brewing inside him. A ray of disgust lengthens across his face.

Then he lifts his head in a slow, tense motion.

I feel quivery, like I've patted myself all over with eucalyptus balm. The sensation is so delicious and cooling. Strangely, I can no longer tell the faces apart at this point—the still one in the portrait and the other bristling in front of me. The similarity comes upon me with a spasm.

It's a *masterpiece*, I gush to myself. Unlike any other I have ever produced.

But Mr. Kwento explodes like a firestorm.

I jump back but lose my footing as he comes at me with the wood-framed portrait. Landing on my back, I roll myself into a ball. He brings the frame down on me. I manage to cushion the blows with my hands.

While he is beating me, I estimate how much I'd make from selling the real portrait I stowed under my bed. Not the one with a rhomb for a head, the ears hanging down from it, eyes carmine and wide apart. Not the one with the nose creased like a bird's anus, pointed cheekbones, and teeth curved over pinkish lips—now tar-black, an inch thicker. Not this caricature that was uglier than all the other caricatures I had done in the past—

that I finished within the wee hours of this morning, which he has now destroyed.

"Filthy pig!" Mr. Kwento sputters, jamming a foot into my kidney.

His kicks pierce my body. I whimper and roll myself up tighter. I try to cradle my hurting ribs, but the pain cuts deeper into my bones.

Machie is screaming hard, though I can't see her. Neither her screaming nor my whimpering stops her husband. His kicks only grow fierce—fiercer than the slap my father dealt me one evening when he caught me in their bedroom slipping some banknotes from my mother's fanny pack. But while my cheek stung from that slap, I sensed the light shift in the room, and my surroundings appeared to be brighter and sharper. I felt strangely soothed and alert. It was as though the slap had brought everything into focus and provided me with a unique perspective on things.

Now, as I buckle about on the ground, I hear the thwack of that slap. I taste its sting of salt and blood on my tongue, and the air wavers and shifts. Everything around me is going to light up in a minute, sharpen into focus.

And this is clarity.

This is redemption.

I think of my mother's kidney, the irony of it all.

And I grin through the clutch of pain, having made out what was hidden behind my neighbour's glossy face.

# BAT

I'm in the kitchen scrubbing the inside of our kettle when I hear my father say, *Bia nwoke*. I dash into the living room while my mother goes on humming over her pot of egusi soup. Each time he summons me, I hear a soldier's voice—hard, sharp, full of bite. But he's not a soldier. Everyone says he fought as a Biafran in the war that happened over thirty years ago. I am only ten, so I don't know if any of that is true. There are no photographs of him in an army uniform anywhere in our apartment, and I have yet to see any terrible scars on his body, like the type on Uncle Iben's face.

I stand in front of my father.

He sits straight in the living room's only armchair. Ever since I saw him flinging his brother out of that chair, I avoid it like sharp spikes poke out of its cushions. Sometime last month, Uncle Iben had staggered back home from a pub, plopped himself in the chair, and ordered to be served like some lord. My father returned from work, dragging his feet along as if he was going to collapse any minute, and saw someone else occupying his throne. He growled and hoisted his brother by the neck. My mother grabbed him by the waist before he could send Uncle Iben flying across the room.

My father sweeps his eyes over me as if I'm dripping suds. "Can the kitchen make a man?" he asks.

I stare at the stump that is his neck. The heave of his large chest. His shoulders are humped. Every time I consider his build, I wonder why he didn't go for a woman his size. He's taller than my mother by two feet.

"Don't look confused. I'm only asking." He points his finger toward the kitchen. He barely moves his head, which seems too small for his stature. "Are you planning to take the kitchen from my wife?"

"No, sir," I reply.

"Then why do you like loitering in the kitchen?"

"I was only helping."

"You act at times like you're not from my sperm."

My mother always looks tired when she returns from Ekeonuwa market, where she goes every day but Sunday to sell ugba. I don't like seeing her like that. But I don't explain this to my father because last Saturday he'd asked me if I wanted to become a woman, and now, he's looking at me like I am one.

He slouches back in his seat, twisting the stubble on his jaw. When I was seven, he would hold my hand and run it against his chin, over the hairs that felt like bristles on my skin. He stopped when I turned ten. I wanted to ask him why, but I didn't because I already knew the answer.

"You're too old to be playing around," he would have said.

"Do you know why I called you in here?" he says now.

I do, but I say no.

He points to the TV. "What are they doing?"

Two sweaty men are tackling each other with all their might. Their faces clench, their muscles pop. Grunting, they try to hurl each other to the floor. A man sporting a white and black striped shirt squirrels endlessly behind them. He darts his head this way and that to see which man will go down first. My father thinks it's fun to watch his fellow men beat each other up.

"They're wrestling."

He cocks his head toward me. "I didn't hear you."

I say it again.

"Are you sure?"

"Yes, sir."

"They're not in the kitchen, are they?"

I say nothing.

My father doesn't repeat his question. Instead, he puts on a grin that reminds me of my friend Izu, who once trapped a bee in a bottle. I had flinched each time the bee slapped around in the bottle, thumping its body against the glass. Izu had filled the bottle with water. We watched the bee floating dead shortly afterwards. That was the third thing I'd seen him kill. The first time, he cut a millipede into three bits with a piece of glass. I could do nothing but watch. The second time it was a frog, which, after crushing its legs, he buried in a hole he had dug.

"I don't want to see you in that bloody kitchen whenever there's a wrestling match on the TV. Do you understand?"

"I hate wrestling."

"What do you know? You better learn to love it."

"I won't."

My reply makes him sit up at once.

"What did you just say?" My father looks both surprised and threatening.

I glance down at my feet.

"I've never slapped you before, you know why?" He pauses long enough to realize that I'm not going to answer him. "The day I slap you, you won't hear a sound in that ear for days. You'll lose some of your teeth, and your mother will have to rush you to the hospital to have them replaced."

My father has never threatened me before. I must have really made him angry. He motions for me to stand in front of him. My knees grow weak. I try not to tremble much. He had once slapped a colleague in his former workplace for calling him *iyan miri*, and the man didn't move his lips properly for two weeks. The words reminded my father of the war and the losses our people suffered, but his boss still went ahead and suspended him for two weeks without pay.

"Chidi," says my father. "Never expect pity from anyone. Life will always try to crush you, so you must toughen up, or else you'll be trampled to dirt. Women are lucky enough because they're the weaker sex. They don't have to be tough. Do you want to be a woman?"

His speech confuses me, so I scrunch my face and stay quiet.

"Let me tell you about my supervisor, who liked to shout at me. Maybe he thought that because I was a dropout, I was just a half-man." He closes his eyes for twenty seconds or so. I wonder why his supervisor would want to insult him. Wasn't he frightened by what my father's knuckles could do? Wasn't he even scared of my father's size?

"One day, I decided to teach him a lesson. Put his mouth in the right place. Do you want to know what happened next?"

I can tell that he expects me to show excitement. But I murmur, "You lost your job."

"If you don't have any bloody brain," he mutters, "at least have some muscles." Raising his beefy left arm, he pumps it so hard his veins tighten and bulge under his skin. It's like the rump of a galloping horse—terrifying to see such a mass of flesh.

Izu would pop his eyes if he were here to see my father rippling the muscles in his biceps. There are times, such as this, that I wonder why my father still works as a loading assistant at a bus station when he could become a wrestler and win many championship belts. If he changed jobs, my mother and I wouldn't have to see him so easily angered and frustrated.

My father grits his teeth. "I suppose your mother is cooking stones, right? How much longer does a man have to wait before he can eat in his own house? Call her."

I spring toward the kitchen.

He calls me back just as I reach the door. His neck seems to enlarge as he adds, "I want to see you here," and clicks his fingers, "in one minute."

I return in less than a minute, puffing. "She's bringing your food."

My father commands me to sit down. "Let's enjoy the wrestling."

*

Two nights before my father dragged me to Izu's place, an ashy thing streaked into our living room and thumped against the TV screen. I jumped in my chair while my mother gasped. The thing lay still. When it jerked across the carpet, my mother scurried out of her seat. I nearly bolted, too, but tried to stay calm when I saw that my father didn't look startled. I couldn't laugh the way he was laughing, though even when he said, "It's only a bloody bat."

"Where did it come from? Where did it come from?" My mother regarded the bat with unease.

My father ignored her. I noticed the slight curl of his lips and wondered if Izu had flung the bat through our window. Although he was mischievous and mean, I didn't think he would dare do such a thing with my father around.

My mother began calling the blood of Jesus. She snapped her fingers, this way and that.

And the bat, as if provoked by the sounds, shot toward the white ceiling. It tipped over in midflight like it had been swatted by an unseen hand.

I folded into myself in fright as it crashed down.

My mother scrambled down the hallway.

Despite its earlier attempts, the bat made to fly a third time but thumped awkwardly to the floor yet again.

My father chuckled hard. I remembered how he had chuckled at his brother. One evening, Uncle Iben had drunkenly staggered into the living room and tumbled over the couch, and my father had called him a "bloody bat."

"Chidi," my mother whispered from the hallway, "get the anointing oil."

My father looked over at her and snickered, "Kasarachi, you want to fry it?"

"Ugh," I said under my breath.

Disgust crossed my mother's face, leaving it pinched. "What if it is a witch?"

"What if it was sent by God?" My father seemed like he wouldn't mind if the bat flapped onto his head.

"God doesn't send witches."

"But He created bats."

My mother glared at him.

Meanwhile, the bat had stopped fumbling.

I tried to will it to rise and vanish, but my father told me to get the bloody mop.

"Sir?"

"Are you deaf?"

Something sharp squeezed my lungs. I wasn't going to move an inch. I hoped the bat was already dead.

"Just kill the witch," said my mother.

The bat screeched, and the sound pinged against my eardrums. It began thrashing again, a blind and helpless thing.

I perched safely in my chair, careful not to wobble or fall off. But I felt weak. I also felt helpless, just as I had when Izu had killed the bee, the millipede, and the frog.

My father bristled and stamped into the bathroom. The echo of his heavy footsteps lingered in the air until he strode back into the living room, wielding the mop. He shot me a piercing look, and I imagined a pair of eyes drilling holes into my head if I held his gaze a second longer. Then he huffed, strode over to me, and wrenched me out of my seat, nearly snapping my thin wrist.

He thrust the mop into my hand.

The hairs on my neck stood on end because I was going to end the bat's life. My wrist hurt as if bitten by pincers.

"*Gbuo ya.*"

I shook my head, wishing I had got the broom instead. I could have swept the bat out of the room.

"Kill it," my father said again.

"Chidi, don't touch it!" cried my mother.

They argued until a clattering sound on the floor jolted her. The mop had slid out of my grasp.

"Pick it up."

"Please let him be."

My father balled his fists, seething. "You won't?"

I wanted to nod my head, but my mother said, "Wait."

I caught a glimpse of her fading from the living room. I couldn't look at him. He was trying hard to hold himself back from striking me, I could tell. This was the first time I'd defied him.

My mother rushed back into the living room with a bottle of Goya. She uncapped it and spilled some olive oil on the bat, which made it beat its little paper wings even harder. She laughed an unkind laugh.

My father gripped my shoulders so powerfully, I felt like my bones would snap.

"Let me tell you, son. I won't always be around to teach you how to be a man. Will you pick up the mop, or not?" he spoke so lightly, but I still made out the razored edge in his voice.

Somehow, I was afraid the bat might scratch out my eyes in terror if I picked it up.

I reached for the mop.

"Finish it."

Izu would have finished the bat off quickly and easily, without hesitation.

"Look at me, Chidi. What would you do if one of those ekunke dogs attacked you?"

My father must have sensed that I wasn't going to budge, so he yanked the mop from my hand. It happened so fast—so fast I didn't even see the mop swing upward. I only heard the cry— short, high-pitched, pained. I couldn't bring myself to look at the remains. The mop was back in the bathroom by the time I blinked.

My father looked at me from head to toe, then shook his head.

*

As my mother positions the food tray on the table, Uncle Iben stumbles in through the front door. The air sours at once. He swings his arms and tries to embrace her, but my mother shrinks away. I don't know why she hasn't yet gotten used to his antics. Not a day has gone by without him returning home like this. His head is shaven so clean that it gleams like a freshly scrubbed marble.

I long to run my fingers over it.

My uncle sees me staring at his head and cracks up. He hardly smiles because of the scar that runs up his chin to his right lip. Each time he pulls a smile, his mouth stretches the wrong way as if to spite him. It's like pulling an elastic coil from both ends.

"Touch it," he says, thrusting his head right under my face.

I wonder how he would react if I rapped my knuckles on it.

"Touch it, touch it."

My father's face is drawn stiff. He tries to appear unruffled while this is going on. Whenever my uncle isn't around, he complains to my mother about his brother crying like a woman, that he doesn't know why Uncle Iben can't fight his way out of his loss, that his cowardice actually puts him off. She often tells him to stop being so hard, to show more sympathy. Grief doesn't care about anyone's looks or size. She's sure he will rise again.

Uncle Iben swipes my hand over his head. It feels so warm, too smooth. I want to close my eyes and soak up the whole warmth. He drops my hand just as suddenly as he grabbed it.

"You like it?" he asks me.

I think of how dry and crackly he looks, like unleavened bread left out in the sun for days. I'd caught him sobbing quietly to himself a few weeks before. But my uncle, a man who used to carry himself like a snail, quiet and unobtrusive, hasn't always been like this. He'd grown miserable, drunk, often disruptive, only after he fled the north for Owerri.

My father had spoken about the terrorists in the north. They had blown up schools, churches, mosques, markets, motor parks, and set many farms on fire. A group had lined up schoolboys and sprayed bullets into their hearts in front of their blazing dormitories. Another group had abducted over a hundred girls. Videos of soldiers beheaded by terrorists circulated on the Internet and people's cellphones. Initially, my father was worried when he couldn't get in touch with his only brother. He didn't stop worrying, especially because no one—not even the government—could keep track of all the people being killed day after day in the north.

Then Uncle Iben appeared one drizzly night.

We were in the living room, praying, when he staggered in, so unexpectedly, that my father forgot his tongue for a few seconds. I'll never forget the way my mother cried upon seeing him at our doorstep. Like he had been dead the whole time and now came to us resurrected. For a whole month, my uncle didn't step outside the veranda. He hid indoors from dawn to dusk. He ate little, spoke no more than four or five words, *Chukwu nyere m aka,* and slept like someone who had overdosed himself. The times I came back from school and ran into him in the hallway, I almost jumped because he was so pale and skinny that any speeding car could have lifted him off his feet and blown him onto the other side of the road.

Eventually, one Saturday morning, Uncle Iben ventured out to town. It was a miracle, I thought. After several hours, he came back at midnight, whooping and humming one of Dr. Sid's songs like he had his pockets full of good news. Since then, he's been drinking with gusto.

"Iben," my father says now, washing his hands in the bowl of water. "Comport yourself."

My uncle swivels around and mumbles, *po-po-po-po pop pop champagne.*

"*O di egwu,*" my mother sighs, pouring some chilled water into the glass.

Once, she tried persuading him to go to church, but he said he would only go if she could tell him where God was when the terrorists butchered his wife and daughter. She hasn't cared to coax him ever since.

My father pretends not to be offended. He moulds a bit of fufu, stirs it in the ofe nsala, and drops it down his throat. He takes a gulp from his glass, then burps.

"Iben, how long will it take you to get over it?"

"Nkem, don't ask me that useless question."

My father tenses up and grips the arms of his chair. His younger brother has never called him by his first name. *Dee* or Brother, my uncle always calls him, never Nkem.

"You think you're stronger than me?" Uncle Iben scoffs.

My father gapes at my mother. He is never mocked. She averts her eyes.

I am sure he has never seen his younger brother act so angry. I'm also sure he will explode. Sometimes, when he has finished watching a wrestling match, he jabs at shadows and dodges invisible blows while whispering *knock him down, knock him over* to himself, over and over again. Whenever I run into him at such moments, I remember how my friends often pestered me with questions: Where does your father keep his machine gun? How many people did he kill during the war? Is it true that he survived five gunshots from the enemy? Even Izu wishes we could swap fathers.

"Iben, if you keep going down this way," my father says, "you may find yourself a wasted man."

My uncle sniffles, then laughs as if his throat is full of syrup. "Preacher Man, I'm tired of all your sermons," he says, jabbing a finger at his own chest. "Don't ever tell me to man up again, or else I'll do something we'll both regret." He waves his arms limply over his head and mimics my father's voice. "Man up. As if that would bring my family back."

A glazed look covers my father's face. He doesn't speak, doesn't look at anyone. He sits there stock-still, clutching a ball of fufu.

My mother starts massaging his shoulders. "Please eat, Nkem," she whispers. "Eat up."

It takes a while before my father moves. He puts the fufu back on the plate and washes his hand again. He doesn't want to eat anymore. He pulls himself out of his chair. Without saying another word, he heads for his room and bangs the door so hard I shiver in my seat.

My mother catches my eye, looking like she has been harassed by a child. I want to ask her if my father has ever beaten up anyone or shot at enemies, but I think I already know the answer. She sighs, picks up the tray, and walks away. She, too, has lost her appetite.

While she is in the kitchen, Uncle Iben wipes his nose with his palm and mutters to himself, "How can I get over it? Did he know I buried my wife and daughter without their heads?"

Before I can sneak out of the room, he breaks down completely.

My mother runs out of the kitchen, afraid a fight might have started, but she stops midway and watches him sob with his head in his hands. She glances over at me, and I know she cannot decide whether to go over and comfort him or not. Then she backs away and goes into their bedroom, leaving me all alone to deal with the bawling adult.

*

Curled up on the veranda, I wince when my father plods back from work. I lower my head, hoping he doesn't notice my wet cheeks. My mother has dabbed some shea butter under my left eye, but it still scalds like pepper. I dry my eyes, though my heartbeat is ringing in my ears. I wish I were somewhere else right now. My father is going to ask me why I'm crying.

Silently, he walks by me. I can't tell what expression he went inside the house with. I hope he is too worn out to ask me questions.

The sun starts to lose colour, and I wish I could hurt Izu back.

I'm about to creep into the living room when I bump into my father. He looms over me, and I feel like an ant. Thick veins rope together in his neck. He points to my face. I have the urge to lie, but he glares at me as if he has read my mind.

"Who did this to you?" He breathes down my neck.

My chest crumples into itself.

My father will explode once he finds out that Izu is to blame for my injury. That braggart's son won't ever come to much good, my father once said. I don't know why he dislikes Mr. Okose, whom everyone considers lucky because he drives the Commissioner for Works around and has bought a Nissan for himself. But Mr. Okose is also the butt of so many colour jokes because his face is mottled from bleaching creams.

"He didn't mean to," I say.

Izu had knowingly punched me in my face while I tried to fight him off from snapping the wings of a sparrow.

"Who didn't mean to?"

"I...Izu..."

"That rascal?" He shoves me forward.

My mother positions herself between both of us.

"Nkem," she says. "Please come in and eat."

"Food can wait," my father tells her in a stern tone. "Let me speak to that bloody ruffian. It's time I taught Chidi how to be a man. We can't have our only child behaving like..." He frowns, maybe because he cannot find the right words to describe me.

"He's wounded, can't you see?"

"You call this a wound? This little swelling?" My father hisses. "I knew soldiers who had lost one eye, and yet they bravely fought off our enemies during the war."

"We are not at war," my mother insists. "And no one has to fight anybody now."

"Life is war. Living is war." He prods under my left eye where it hurts.

I grind my teeth to stop myself from howling in pain.

"You'll only hurt him more!" my mother cries, slapping him on the wrist.

"He is my son. I can hurt him any way I like." My father shoves me forward again, toward our gate. "But only I can hurt my son."

She pleads with him. "*E ji m chukwu rio gi,* I don't want any fight."

"I don't like the way you talk at times, Kasarachi. I'm now a fighter, eh? Is it when they've damaged his eye and we are left with a blind boy that you'll have me act?"

My mother lifts her arms in defeat. She gives him a harsh look before stomping away. I wish Izu hadn't injured me just because of that stupid bird that had landed on the steps beside us.

A few minutes later, my father and I are standing in front of a two-storey building with walls the colour of a tortoiseshell. Izu and his parents live on the street right behind ours.

"Is this where that tadpole lives?" he asks me, motioning to the rusted gate.

Why is he acting as though he doesn't know Izu lives here? Everyone knows that Mr. Okose occupies the first apartment on the ground floor facing the gate. I can't shake off the feeling that my father might have been practising ahead of this moment.

Something grips my heart as he pounds the door with his fist. All those times I had seen him shadowboxing had prepared him for this.

*"Onye?"* a man hollers from inside.

My father snorts and bangs harder. The bulb in the veranda comes on, a garish white.

I pray that Izu's parents will behave themselves, so my father doesn't get more provoked and pick Izu's father off his feet and toss him against their door. I wouldn't feel proud if he beat up someone's father. I already feel embarrassed when I'm pointed at in the neighbourhood, referred to as the boy whose father is an *ex-soldier.* That Biafran man.

The door flies open.

Mr. Okose stamps out of his living room in khaki shorts and a white singlet. His filmy face is clenched in anger, but it grows soft the instant he recognizes my father. His wife appears behind him, fluttering like a fat owl in daylight. The Okoses probably didn't think they would find him towering in their doorway.

I've noticed the same look on some neighbours' faces any-time they come across my father. He keeps to himself and does not attend any events organized in our street, so people hold him in awe.

"Good evening, Mr. Nkem."

"Is your boy in?" My father refuses the pleasantries.

"Hope there's no problem, my good neighbour?"

"Your boy wants to damage my son's eye."

*"Eewo,"* Mrs. Okose cries and jostles her husband aside. She squats in front of me, rather carelessly, so her breasts spill half-way out of her low-neck blouse.

I quickly look over her shoulder.

She rubs my head as if I'm her baby, speaking in a rushed sing-song voice, *"Ndo, ndo."*

An image of the wrestling match flashes through my head. This is the moment my father will jab Mr. Okose in the belly. The moment he will repeat to himself, *knock him down, knock him over.*

It seems Mr. Okose's face will tear easily from one sweep of his knuckles. Watching it twitch as he speaks, I think he is nervous already. He expresses himself a little too fast. His eyes scuttle this way and that as if to keep up with my father's words. I imagine a crab running helter-skelter the second it lands in a pot of hot water.

"Where's that problem child?" Mrs. Okose stops rubbing my head. "Izu!"

Izu skips around the corner, halting abruptly when he sees us.

My father narrows his eyes at him.

My chest tightens. I remember the bat he had killed two nights ago. What if he tells me to strike Izu in front of his parents?

Meanwhile, Izu looks like he's going to shrink into himself as his father grabs him by the ear, swings him round, and raps his knuckles hard on his head. Deep, spastic sounds burst from Izu's throat. He howls as though he wants to cough up all his insides. He rubs his sore head with both hands.

I avoid his eyes as his father vows that he will be using a belt on him afterwards. I feel bad watching him cry. I am not sure I want to get even anymore.

"We're sorry for all the trouble," Mr. Okose says. "But why not come into our house, let us apologize properly over some whisky?"

"I can prepare some ugba in a few seconds," his wife chips in.

My father looks at her and shakes his head. "It's late."

The couple exchange glances. Then Mrs. Okose brushes her son aside and runs into their apartment. Mr. Okose's washed-out face takes on a shine like he's tipsy. He cajoles my father to visit their humble home anytime.

When his wife returns, her face slick with sweat, he repeats those words. In her hand is a wide-bottomed green bottle of wine, which looks delicate and costly. She is about to hand it over to my father when her husband tells her to wait. Confusion flickers across her face. Mr. Okose snatches the bottle from his wife and holds it out to my father with both hands.

"My good neighbour, for you," he says, smiling. "Our door is open, anytime, anytime."

My father frowns at them. There is a moment of silence, and I can't tell what he is thinking right now. It seems like Mrs. Okose will drop to her knees if he holds her gaze a minute longer. He is looking at her like there's something he finds unflattering about her—something oily about her round face. He turns to her husband and takes the bottle stiffly by the neck. He taps me on the shoulder and hands the bottle to me.

Without saying thank-you or goodbye, my father strides out the gate.

Mr. Okose calls after him, reminding him to extend his warmest greetings to my mother.

My father does not reply or glance back.

In the cobalt sky, the moon bares its fullness. Like yolk, too yellow and unreal. Something, probably a bat, shrieks over-head, and my father begins to hum a tune that my mother likes humming whenever she is in the kitchen. I hurry after him, surprised that he didn't strike the neighbours. Surprised he didn't ask me to hit Izu. Maybe that's what my father meant when he tells me I must learn to be a man.

# DOUBLE WAHALA

Chux sends one of the pillows flying across the bedroom with a sweep of his hand. He grabs the blanket and flings it to the floor. He stamps into the living room, heaves the couch to one side, and looks underneath. He lets the couch drop with a thud. How can a bag of money vanish? He sinks to his knees, his heart thumping in his ears, and clasps his hands over his mouth. No, this can't be happening.

Chux gets up and starts rifling through the cushions. He turns around, and his shin connects with the edge of the centre table. He howls in pain and, hobbling around the table, slumps backwards onto the couch. Leaning forward, he grabs the table by its leg and flips it. He thinks of dragging the table outside and ramming an axe through it. But Somto will think he's mad. Hasn't she driven him mad already?

Relief seeps through Chux as he rolls up his pants—his skin isn't scraped. He rolls his pants back down, glances upward, and notices dust on the ceiling. Somto can't pretend that she hasn't seen it. Why hasn't she brushed it clean? She spends every other Saturday cleaning the church, so why can't she keep their home spotless?

Chux glares at the cracks between the dust patches. The ceiling is drooping. Everything in the building is rotting. What's he even paying for if there are all these damages? His wicked landlord is only interested in demanding his rent. The old goat had yelled several times through their door: *Where is my rent? I'll call thugs to throw you out!*

"I'm going to give that *ewu* a piece of my mind." Chux fumes.

As he tears his gaze from the ceiling, he thinks the holy face in the framed picture on the wall is smirking at him. He smirks back at it and rights the table back on its legs. He has scattered the bedroom and living room. Overturned everything. Upside down. But he still can't find the bag of money anywhere.

Upside down.

Chux remembers the woman on the radio show and how the crusade idea came to him. He had been sitting squashed on the rickety bus while a woman on the radio begged the preacher to pray for her because *everything in her life was upside down*. He knew then, upon hearing those words, how best to solve his rent problems.

Chux stands and goes to the backyard. He falls to his knees, scans the grass. No ashes, no paper shreds. Nothing, except the sound of Fela screaming, "Double Wahala!" on the other side of the wall. The song vexes Chux, causing his brow to tighten. Feeling more frustrated than ever, he marches back into the living room, his fists clenched, ready to strike anyone in his way. He drops himself onto the couch, breathing hard. He grips his head with both hands, fingers clawing at his scalp. He feels as if he is about to choke. He wants to scream but fears that his lungs will explode.

Chux springs from the couch again and dashes out to the front of the building. The breeze envelopes him and fills him with warmth. He tries to breathe slowly as he stands at the compound gate and looks around the street. Everything seems calm and normal, except that he can't find the money he thought he'd stashed under the bed.

Fifteen thousand eight hundred and ninety naira couldn't just vanish. Chux closes his eyes briefly, breathes out, then stumbles back into his apartment. Three weeks before, he and Lemchi were sitting on the steps of the unfinished building behind his compound, both trying to learn some Bible passages by heart. He hadn't known then that Somto would make a mess of their plan.

"*Nwanna*, we need to memorize everything."

"Receive it, receive your anointing!" Lemchi mimicked a voice.

"Have you talked with the printer?" Chux asked.

"Ah, Jesus wept." Lemchi yawned. "Yes, we agreed on the price. One hundred copies will do."

Now, what would he tell Lemchi? That the money was gone? Lemchi wouldn't believe him. Chux recalls how they had once posed as local government officials and sold fake stickers to drivers on Tetlow Road. A police officer had appeared from nowhere, and they had scampered off in fear of being caught. Later, he discovered that a part of the money had slipped out from a hole in his pocket. Lemchi had never believed the story. Chux, he'd thought, had intentionally cut the pocket.

"I'm dead." Chux slaps his head with both hands, dreading his friend's reaction.

After all the trouble of planning the crusade. He should have halved the money and given Lemchi his own share. He should have worried less, like his friend, who never took anything seriously. While he worried about the crusade, Lemchi had hung out with girls at pubs and clubs. He later came up with the idea of Mt. Jericho Anointing Oil. Chux had doubted that anyone would pay a kobo for such a tiny bottle, but his friend had pasted colourful stickers of smoky mountains on each of the eight hundred bottles in the four cartons. The night they executed their plan, Chux stomped across the podium, rapping and reeling out a crazed language while the villagers, thinking the oil had originated from Israel, jostled each other to grab a bottle.

Chux glares over at the picture of St. Boniface on the wall, and his anger heightens. Every few weeks, Somto stroked the glassy face of the saint as though it were her own soft cheek. He wishes she stroked him the way she did the picture. He gets up, yanks the picture from the nail, and hurls it against the wall.

Shards fly.

An eye for an eye!

Her precious totem is gone, just like his money.

An hour later, Chux jerks awake on the couch at the sound of the door slamming. He had drifted off and hadn't heard the door open. His violent outbursts must have drained him. Now he stares at Somto as she walks past without even saying hello.

She doesn't notice yet that he has destroyed her picture of St. Boniface. She will go mad once she sees it is no longer there on the wall. She is joyfully singing a gospel song. How had she found the money under their bed? She hadn't been home when he hid it there.

Chux jumps from the couch.

"Where's the money?" He latches onto her shoulders.

Somto twists her neck sideways. He wrenches her around to face him.

"What did you do with the money?"

She lifts her hand to her cheek to wipe at the spit that accompanied his question.

What has gotten into her? Somto has never defied him before. It must have something to do with her church. Lemchi doesn't have to put up with this kind of shit. Beer. Girls. And parties. That was all he was about. A single man at forty. Chux drops his hands from her shoulders.

Somto turns around, and as she starts walking to the kitchen, he spots the black plastic bag in her hand and runs after her. He makes a grab for it, but she sidesteps him, and he swipes at air.

"Give it to me." He swipes again.

Quietly, she hands the bag to him.

He peers inside.

Ukazi? Onions? Ede? Meat?

Soup items.

He drops the bag on the floor and sees her grinning.

"Woman, I'm not joking," Chux snaps at her. "Where's my money?!"

"*Your* money?" Somto says. "Blood money, you mean." She bends over, picks up the bag, and lays it on the countertop. "I gave it all to my church. The Apostle will hand it over to a charity home after he's done praying on it. After all, you and I decided not to keep it, didn't we?"

Chux remembers her threat two nights before: *Return it, or I pack my things and leave your house with my children.* He isn't sure he consented to either option; he'd remained quiet. At the time, he hadn't wanted to fight in front of the kids. Besides, he was still giddy over the operation he and Lemchi had pulled off, so she might have misread his silence.

"Prophet Jeremy?" Somto had spat.

She'd found out what he and Lemchi had done two days after their crusade, waving their poster of him wielding a large Bible and gazing into heaven.

Chux had stared disbelievingly at her, wondering how she had found the poster. She told him how Mama Atta Boy had seen it at the gate of a school while waiting for a bus to return her to the city. She doubted the woman at first but went along anyway to see if it was true. As Lemchi had suggested, the print was a bit blurred—deliberately—so none of their friends or relatives would easily identify their faces. To further reduce their chances of getting recognized, they had pasted the posters on the outskirts of Owerri.

"You've turned me into a professional liar," she had accused him.

"How?" he'd stuttered.

Somto had looked him up and down. "I lied," she blurted. "I had to lie, to save myself from shame. Our family from shame. Shame! Something you no longer have in you!"

Chux remembers what Somto had told Mama Atta Boy: "My husband is not a serious Christian, so that can't be him."

"You gave my money to your church?" he yells now, gripping her wrist.

"My church is a more honourable cause than you," she replies coolly.

He almost yanks the scarf off her head. The tatty scarf that gives her an annoying righteous look. Instead, he tightens his grip some more.

Somto pulls. "You're hurting me. Let go."

Chux shoves her aside and stamps off to the washroom. He flings the door open, swearing to get the money back from the Apostle, no matter what it takes. Apostle, my arse. As Chux pulls down his fly and pees into the bowl, he hears the rumble of a car outside. He recognizes the sound. It is his landlord's Volvo.

The goat always sounds his horn to announce his presence at the gate. He wants the entire neighbourhood to know that he's around. He also enjoys blasting his horn just to terrify his tenants. Typical big man.

Chux peeps out the window and draws back at once. For an instant, he considers locking himself in the washroom. Then he zips up fast.

Somto is singing a song by Patty Obasi and cutting spinach on a board, when Chux sneaks back into the kitchen.

"It's him," he whispers, glancing over his shoulder as if the landlord had trailed him.

"*Onye?*" she asks.

"Landlord. Let him know I've travelled."

"I can't keep lying for you," Somto protests.

Chux thinks of shaking her shoulders till her teeth rattle and telling her that she has to lie if she wants to keep living here. After all, she contributes very little to the family's upkeep, what with her useless job of babysitting children at the church.

Frustration makes him want to rip down the shelf of tableware. He remembers his landlord's threat.

"Travel," Chux had whispered to Somto, handing her his phone, two weeks ago. She had frowned and shaken her head. He pleaded with her, and then she pressed the phone to her ear.

"So sorry, sir," she'd said to the landlord. "Baby was crying. My husband is travelling." After speaking to the goat, she told Chux about his threats: if they didn't pay their rent by the month's end, all their belongings would be thrown away.

Chux had called his bluff then. But the landlord is already out there now, ready to tear him to pieces. What is he going to do? He dashes back into the washroom, twisting the key in the lock. He leans his back against the door, panting. Any moment now, Lemchi will appear too. Chux jumps as fists pound on the front door. He hasn't paid his rent for the last four months. It isn't his fault; his landlord is a heartless goat.

Around last Christmas, the goat had come barking: *Mister, I've rearranged rent payments. Every tenant is to pay in two instalments. The first instalment in January, the second in July. Six months' rent apiece.* Chux had contained himself from hitting out at him. Perhaps he should step out and do it now. Lemchi is lucky, he thinks. His landlord has a better arrangement where tenants pay their rent monthly.

Chux glares at the tiled wall and sees a reflection of himself dressed up in a police uniform, banging at someone's door in Prefab Estate—a man who had intimidated Lemchi's girlfriend. More images surge into his head. The car dealer with connections across the Seme border, the engineer who supervised a flow station in Egbema, and other spurious characters he and Lemchi had played over six years—after Gibbs Enterprises, an auto service company, had laid him off for stealing two drums of diesel. His favourite scam was when Lemchi acted as an airport taxi driver, and Chux disguised himself as a Gabonese businessman.

"Sir, I can get you a translator, if you wish," Lemchi had said, just as a man was sliding next to Chux in the backseat of the car.

"*Oui? Merci, merci,*" Chux replied, nodding. "*Mon ami,* you know, buyer, who I sell market for sodium hydroxide?"

Lemchi's eyes popped in the rear-view window. "You sell hydroxide?"

Chux reached for his briefcase. "Me, plenty in Gabon, Selenium *beaucoup*. Original shipment from France. *Très beaucoup*. Plenty chemicals for printing money, me sell to you, *c'est?*" He then slipped out a small bottle with "Sodium Hydroxide" written in bold cursive over it. The passenger, who had been listening intently, showed interest and later lived to regret his greed.

The banging on the front door persists, rattling the washroom window. A lizard drops from the sill and scuttles through the opening under the door.

Chux hears Somto scream out, "I'm coming!" and regrets not going to entreat the landlord beforehand, as she'd advised. But the last time he'd visited him to discuss his rent, the goat had turned up his nose as though he and his family stank.

Chux leans over to spit and catches sight of a yellow blob in the washroom bowl. He pulls back, wrinkling his nose. This is it, huh? His life has been reduced to shit ready to be flushed down the drain.

Chux becomes angry with his children's inattention. How many times must he drum it into their ears? He had warned them to stop using the washroom since the tap hardly ran. *Go behind the unfinished building and do your business there.* Apparently, nobody takes him seriously any longer, not even his wife, whose life he's struggling to make better.

Somto's scream jolts him back to reality.

The goat must have hired a couple of thugs to rough handle him and his wife.

Chux unbolts the door, darts out, and sees Somto wrestling the TV set from the grasp of a shirtless young man. Two other men shove the battered couch through the door. Chux turns as his wife thumps to the floor. The man scurries out through the door with the TV, chuckling like a bush fowl.

Chux reaches out a hand to lift Somto to her feet, but she slaps it away.

"Do something," she sobs.

For a moment, her teary face reminds Chux of all the people he had swindled and the women whose hearts he had broken, even the ones who threatened to send killers after him, or the one who brought the police to handcuff him—although he got his bail without much delay because some of the officers were his drinking buddies—and even the ones who took his name to the Okija shrine, so the gods could maim him or render him impotent.

Chux helps Somto get up, then stamps out of the living room and into the yard.

"Ha, that's the debtor," the landlord exclaims, swaggering over to him.

Chux's possessions are scattered all over the grass. He longs to swat at the landlord's chubby nose, but he imagines himself stretched out like a lizard on the ground, a thug's large foot crushing his spine. He longs to humiliate his landlord one way or another. He would enjoy seeing his face droop. But he is at the mercy of the goat right now.

The landlord smirks at him.

Chux makes to leave, afraid that he might deal the goat a blow if he doesn't restrain himself.

"I'm not through with you yet."

Chux pauses, narrowing his eyes. He is about to spit out his own threats when they both swing their heads toward a Honda rocketing at them. The car pitches to a sudden halt next to the landlord's Volvo, almost clipping the outside mirror.

The landlord swivels around sharply and marches toward the car, probably to tell the Honda driver off for parking so close to his own car. The door opens slowly, and Lemchi slides out, dapper in a V-neck shirt, cargo shorts, and loafers. He strides past the landlord, paying him no attention.

Chux wants to smile but panic seizes him. Lemchi will never forgive him once he discovers that their crusade money is gone.

"That's the car I was telling you—" Lemchi starts to say.

"Do as I say," Chux cuts him short.

Lemchi tilts his head sideways. "What?"

"My landlord, you know him."

"What about the money?" Lemchi insists, looking impatient. "Jessy and I need it now."

Chux stiffens as the landlord moves toward them.

"We're in trouble," he whispers to Lemchi as the footsteps draw nearer.

"Mister, it's time to say, how do you put it?" the landlord says out loud as though to impress Lemchi with his presence and voice. "Good riddance to bad rubbish, right? Ha, ha."

Then he heaves his bulk away, swaggering into the compound to ensure his eviction orders are thoroughly carried out.

Lemchi frowns. "I thought we were supposed to meet this morning?"

"Sir!" Chux cries out. "Wait."

The landlord turns around at the gate.

"May I introduce you to my lawyer," Chux says, patting Lemchi on the shoulder, hoping his friend will play along. "He wants to have a word with you."

The landlord eyeballs him, then Lemchi. "What rubbish are you talking about?"

Before Chux can reply, his children sprint into view. Their schoolbags dangle from their shoulders, swaying back and forth. Chux shivers.

"Daddy. Daddy, look!" Flocking behind him, the three kids point at the messy pile of cutlery and clothing and furniture strewn across the earth.

Chux hears Lemchi clear his throat. Fear grips him. In a flash, he sees the disgrace that awaits him. He is going to be the laughingstock of the entire neighbourhood in a minute. Sweat pools in his armpits as Lemchi walks up to the landlord.

"Nobody is threatening anybody," his friend says, with professional calm.

The landlord snorts. "And who are you?"

"Call me Barrister Madu. But that's inconsequential."

"This has nothing to do with you. This is my property. I can threaten anybody living here."

"Go ahead and threaten the world," Lemchi says, sweeping his arm in the air. "You're just the kind of person I like dragging before the law. Our judges can be crazy, you know. Especially about women's rights, child abuse. Did you hear about Justice Ekezie's verdict? The one about the landlord who caused a female tenant to miscarry? Oh, well, never mind. You don't seem to keep up with the news, do you? I can only assume you've nothing against mothers and children. Our judges, eccentric folks. Hmm. I wonder why they get sentimental when it comes to cases involving women's rights and poor kids young enough to be one's grandchildren, or assault—or is it battery? The law is an ass, they say. You know what I think, Mr. I-Can-Threaten-Anyone?" Lemchi pauses, smiles.

A shadow crosses the landlord's face.

"You really want to know?" Lemchi continues. "I don't think so."

The landlord scowls at him, balling his fists.

Chux tries to smile, but Lemchi shoots him a severe look, then turns back to the landlord. "The tree doesn't forget the axe. I promise you. I'll meet you in court whenever you're ready."

"I'll be back," the landlord threatens and storms past them into the compound, calling his men to a stop.

"We'll be waiting for you, sir," Chux shouts after him, laughing.

As the two friends walk into the compound, Lemchi puts an arm over Chux's shoulders and says, "So, where's my money, Prophet Jeremy?"

# WILD FLAMES

## 1.

We heard loud voices outside the windows, and then a scream rang through the air. Papa, Mama, and I rushed out of our rooms. The sky was on fire. Smoke seethed through the air. It wasn't yet dawn, but the street buzzed with confusion. Our neighbours screamed and cried. I thought another pipeline had exploded and our farmlands were burning, just like nine years ago. Firefighters from Germany had flown in then and stopped our village from turning to ash. Westoil had been to blame. I wondered if they were involved in this one too.

People raced back and forth with water buckets, trying to put out the flames that roared in Bobo's father's building. I clamped a hand over my nose and mouth. Bobo's mother rolled on the ground. A few women tried to calm her, but she continued to thrash and wail. Her husband looked like he was carved out of a rock, too shocked to even open his mouth.

I looked around for Bobo but couldn't see him. Papa hovered on the veranda, then went to help with the fire. Mama, her face twisted in horror, stood with the rest of the women.

"Who could have done this?" a woman asked.

"It was Jachi," another replied. "Only God will deliver us from that *agwuisi*."

An old woman shrieked dolefully and slapped her thigh. "That boy is a disease."

The rest of The Brothers crowded around me.

"Has anybody seen Bobo?" I asked.

"He's dead,"' Uzzi said.

Those words chilled my bones. The air was stifling hot, but my hands quaked. I waited for one of my friends to say Uzzi was kidding, but no one spoke. I studied their faces one by one, each of them struggling with words. Just the night before, Bobo and I had eaten nkwobi at Madam Sunshine's, which sold bush meat, pepper soup, palm wine, and alcohol. Madam Sunshine's pub was a short distance from Westoil's buildings.

"Was it the fire?" I asked.

"He was clubbed first," Uzzi mumbled.

"And then burned to death," added Danny. "Those bastards."

I reeled and dropped to my knees. Slammed a fist into the ground. Bobo wasn't supposed to die like that, so easily, so horribly. His ideas had only begun to grow. In less than a year, he had made our village safe again from Jachi's gang.

We all ducked when we heard a boom. It sounded like gunfire, but it was only thunder. Lightning slashed the deep grey sky. The rain came down, hard as pebbles. This was a relief, at least, for the burning building. It began to put out the fire. Everybody first stood still as the rain poured, until one of the women broke from the crowd and scurried for shelter. The others immediately moved as well.

Mama screamed my name.

The Brothers decided to meet at dawn.

## 2.

Papa scolded me as soon as I entered the room. He puffed furiously on his cigarette. I thought it was strange that he was smoking after a fire incident.

"That could have happened to us," he said and blew cigarette smoke toward me.

Mama sat close, gnashing her teeth.

"Woman," Papa hissed. "Stop that noise."

Mama went still. I wasn't listening to Papa. I was thinking about Bobo, how he'd rallied us against Jachi.

Papa's words broke off my thoughts. "I've warned you before. I'm warning you again. I will look the other way if anything bad happens to you. Now get lost before I crack your skull!"

I jutted out my chin.

Papa threw his cigarette at me. "I'll pluck out your eyes if you look at me like that."

I turned and stamped into my room. Mama came after me. I flopped down on the bed, and she sat next to me. She and Papa had often warned me to stop hanging out with The Brothers. The devil's workers, Mama had labelled them. She'd long ago pleaded with me to go and live with her elder sister in Abakaliki. She believed if I enrolled in the same school as my cousins, I could pass the exams that I had failed several times.

Mama's eyes flitted up and down as she spoke. "Kalu, you are our only child. For heaven's sake, do not allow *ekwensu* to use you as his tool." She clasped my right hand and sighed. "Have you taken a blood oath? Can you not see the pit before your feet?"

I put an arm over her shoulders. "Mama, you worry too much."

"I worry just enough. I carried you in my womb. You want to get yourself killed?" Mama jiggled her legs. Her breathing was uneven, tense like a cord waiting to snap.

Outside, the rain hammered the rooftops. Darkness hung heavy. Daylight wouldn't arrive for a while. I pictured what was left of Bobo lying in that desiccated building and shuddered.

Mama got up. "I hope this teaches you a lesson." And she left the room.

I stretched out on the bed. Death held an axe over our heads, the remaining members of The Brothers. What I had once fancied seemed dangerous now. Maybe Mama was right. Was it time I left the village? No, Bobo had taught me to be brave. He had known the day of bloodshed was coming. I'd been fighting off sleep lately because I didn't want to be caught off guard. I would rather Jachi's gang break into our house, and I could plunge my dagger into their necks, one after the other. I often lay on the floor by the window to watch for any sign of danger. Our rivals had become deadlier than the gas eating our lungs. Anyone who spoke out against them got beaten. Or killed.

Jachi was tall and beefy, the kind of boy you'd see at night and your heartbeat would quicken until he had walked past you and disappeared from the street. His face was smooth and oval, framed by pretty sideburns. I hated how he flaunted himself everywhere. He was a college dropout. A nobody. Unlike Bobo, who had brought us together. The Brothers, a group of seven boys, were determined to protect what was left of our land, which oil spills had disfigured.

### 3.

We never used to have any factions. Not until May 2006, when it all started with a few boys who loved extorting money from Westoil engineers. Their parents lived along a dirt road, close to one of the oil heads. The road was bumpy, rarely used except by motorcyclists and Westoil trucks. Erosion had chopped off most of the road and it turned into a marsh when it rained. As soon as the boys heard Westoil trucks approach the road, they would storm out with cutlasses and mount a roadblock.

The engineers were always frightened since they weren't indigenes, and they ended up parting with their money every time. They didn't want to stoke the tensions between the village and the company. Except for a few villagers, everybody hated

Westoil and the state governor for leaving the land so scarred and sooty. The extortion would continue for months until one morning, in August 2006, when the engineers sat back in their offices and refused to move an inch near the oil head unless someone dealt with the boys.

## 4.

That was when Jachi entered the scene, or how two crooks brought him into the picture. The story is that an elder had met with a British manager at the staff club of Westoil. In half an hour, Chief Uka and Mr. Laggard had hatched up a plan against the local "miscreants." No one knew for sure how much of the story was true, but that was how it was told.

## 5.

Jachi went by himself to see the boys the following week. All but one of them ran off into the bush, and Jachi flicked out a knife and stabbed the remaining boy in the chest.

## 6.

Westoil engineers went back to work on that site without any more incidents. No one ever complained of extortion again. And everything, for a while, appeared calm. Then some plain-clothes men visited our village. Jachi, who was guzzling palm wine at Madam Sunshine's, found himself behind bars. People thought he would spend a long time there for having almost killed a fellow youth. But Jachi came out after two days and sped through the village on a motorcycle. His friends welcomed him home like a war hero, with plenty of girls and beer. That evening, at his parents' house, he threw a party that lasted till dawn.

## 7.

Nobody heard of Jachi again until another gang charged through Westoil premises. This was in March 2007. Armed with cutlasses, the gang rounded up most of the staff and kept them hostage until Mr. Laggard and his colleagues came out to negotiate with them. The gang was invited to the boardroom. After lengthy discussions, its members demanded two million naira as compensation for the damages Westoil had caused in Egbema. Westoil had to pay the amount or shut down its operations in our village. Mr. Laggard assured them he would contact the headquarters. They gave him three days and stormed out of the premises.

## 8.

Those three days passed, and nothing happened. No money appeared. The gang had issued a threat without teeth. The air was so grim that the elders spoke very little. Everyone was afraid of what might happen next. No group had served Westoil an ultimatum before. An armed force drove its truck into our village on the sixth day after the negotiation. We learned later on that Westoil had sworn not to give in to "local terrorists" and instead deployed armed personnel to guard its headquarters. The state governor vowed "to restore sanity" in Egbema.

Operations smoothly continued.

The gang mailed reminders to Mr. Laggard. Weeks passed. Not one reply returned. Two weeks later, the gang attacked

Westoil shortly after midnight. They tied up the armed personnel with sisal ropes and gathered all the guns. The gang secured
the gates from the inside with padlocks and chains, so no staff
could enter or exit. The night crew couldn't get home when
dawn came. The day shift couldn't get in, either. They camped
outside the gates.

A chopper whirred overhead later in the day. Executives
from Lagos had landed with briefcases. The gang unlocked
the smaller gate to let them in, insisting its members wouldn't
leave without the money. Negotiations took place once more in
the boardroom. The captives were released, and everyone went
home. This time, the gang received their funds.

Life turned into a party for its members, and they became the
talk of the town. They were popular at pubs and hotels. Bought
cars and cruised from one end of the village to another. Music
boomed from their speakers, punctuated by wild laughter. They
wore the flashiest designer clothes and the trendiest shoes and
sneakers. Sometimes they competed amongst themselves to see
who could sleep with the most girls.

Their spoils dried up before long. The gang went broke and
started harassing oil workers again, assaulting girls who ignored
them, and striking boys who dared to speak against them. Its
members became uncontainable, like a virus outbreak.

## 9.

Our king, the Eze, looked helpless when Mr. Laggard said
the boys must be contained or Westoil would stop its operations.
The Eze had never suffered such indignity from his citizens
before. No youths had ever terrorized the village so openly. After
Mr. Laggard left the palace with his aides, Chief Uka appeared in
the doorway, a bottle of wine and a pouch of kolanuts in hand.
Most of the details about their meeting remained a secret, but
everyone said that Chief Uka had persuaded the Eze to approve a
vigilante group to "get this whole madness in check."

## 10.

The unrest ceased, and fear finally died down once the gang members were attacked. People went about their business. The gang would trouble the village no more. A new group had pounced on them on their way to the Westoil premises and over-powered them. Two boys had bled to death in the fracas, their skulls cracked open. The gang's remaining members, severely wounded and bound up, were handed over to the police. Every villager was happy—or so it seemed—that Jachi had orchestrated the calm.

## 11.

With support from Westoil, Chief Uka hired Jachi to head the newly- formed vigilantes. He got his friends together to set up lookout posts. Soon, reports of boys being roughened up and girls having their breasts squeezed circulated around the village. The Eze sent for Jachi, who promised that he would caution his members. In the end, his vigilantes took to play-ing draughts most mornings, drinking most afternoons, and womanizing most nights. There were no more complaints, except for a few cases of missing poultry or cutlery.

## 12.

Jachi paraded himself as the Youth President and obtained numerous opportunities to attend meetings within and outside Egbema. He visited other oil-producing states. In less than two years, he had travelled to more than thirteen cities. Whenever he returned from such trips, he would distribute a variety of

spirits and wines to the Eze, the elders, and his benefactor—
Chief Uka. Once, the federal government hosted youth from
the Niger Delta region in Abuja, and Jachi was among the
invitees. He came back chanting, "Oil communities are the
golden eggs of the nation!"

Jachi made loads of money from his position and registered a
company that supplied materials and labour to Westoil. He grew
close to Mr. Laggard, and they both drank together on weekends.
Jachi bought his parents a second-hand Toyota Hatchback and a
BMW 5 series for himself. Boys and girls buzzed like bees around
him. He oozed money wherever he went.

It was during that period I suffered my first heartbreak. I
found out that he'd been sleeping with my girlfriend. I con-
fronted Chinwe, but she flatly denied it, and later that day
she dumped me. Meanwhile, many villagers grumbled that the
Eze was going to confer a chieftaincy title on Jachi during the
upcoming Easter celebrations. It sounded sacrilegious, like an
elder had lost his senses and shat out in the open.

But then Bobo came back from Enugu, where he had been
studying pharmacy at the university, and everything turned
upside down for Jachi. Or rather, everything turned upside
down for everyone in our village.

## 13.

After Jachi killed Bobo, silence gripped every home. The
Brothers had met at dawn, like we'd planned. We knew what
we had to do. The following Friday, we attended Bobo's burial
dressed in black, our heads shaved and shiny like glass. Bobo's
parents sat in stillness among grieving relatives. Their son's
murderers were in hiding, and we knew nothing about their
whereabouts. I couldn't believe the remains in the coffin were
our leader. I felt a flame was trapped in my chest and I longed

to smash anything in sight. My tongue tasted of ash, but I tried not to vomit.

I swallowed the bitter saliva that flooded my mouth. Why hadn't they closed the coffin during the prayers? Bobo's sister, Oge, and I stared at each other with longing before I left the burial. She wasn't my girlfriend, but I'd planned to make her mine. She was small, always smiling her gap-toothed smile, and her eyes danced like a gentle wind. But now, her face was crumpled. Her lips were cracked. If I could only hug her.

"No one in Jachi's family will find peace ever again," Uzzi promised.

We had appointed him as our next leader. He was fearless and squat, a fellow with a bulbous nose. He had catlike reflexes and could slam you on the ground before you even reached out to touch him. He had trained to be an electrician but worked as a security guard at a lumber mill. He left that job after five or six months to take up hunting for and trading junk.

A week after Bobo's burial, we visited Jachi's house. The sun needled my neck and scorched the earth. His parents sat on a bench on their veranda, enjoying the breeze. His other siblings were nowhere in sight. As we fell upon the parents, they begged and bawled like babies. We grabbed the old man, shoved him down. Snot flowed out of his wife's nose as she cried for mercy. We dragged her by the hair and flung her to the ground next to her husband.

I lobbed spit at them.

We yanked branches off trees and flogged them. Their cries didn't affect any of us. We raided the house, hauled out their belongings, and emptied a gallon of gasoline on the heap. A bonfire crackled and devoured its way toward the house.

We spotted the Toyota Hatchback parked under a mango tree. Smashed the windows. Slashed the tires. Everything was on fire. We whooped as we visited the other gang members' houses next, one after the other. We beat up whoever we found there, man or woman; it didn't matter. We brought out our gas-oline and matchbox and turned each property into a bonfire.

We stomped our feet in dance, howling like wolves.

"Bring it on."

"Yes, let hell come!"

We hooted as we headed straight for Chief Uka's mansion. The news of our retaliation had begun to spread throughout the village. People ducked out of sight. We brandished our machetes as we sang and swayed on the street. We were like the Bakassi Boys, the vigilantes dreaded across the southeast, only that we didn't behead criminals.

Chief Uka had vanished by the time we arrived at his com-pound. We did not think about his so-called juju as we cast his wives and daughters outside. We battered the cars and burned everything we could find in his house. By the time we got to the Westoil premises, not even a rat could be found there. Some boys already had hacked down the company's billboard that promised "10,000 jobs for today's youth."

## 14.

In the days that followed, we found out that everyone was pleased with our actions. Many villagers took The Brothers for heroes. Little children ran after us, shouting: "Brother, brother, carry me!" Girls giggled when we winked at them. Other boys thrust up their fists in solidarity. Mothers greeted us fondly like we were their sons-in-law. Old men nodded at us.

What could be more empowering than that kind of esteem?

We didn't let any of it get to our heads. Neither did we bask in the victory. We only felt the same way you'd feel after you had rid a path of rubbish.

## 15.

Papa avoided speaking to me and didn't return my greetings. Mama acted like she wouldn't mind biting off my ear. She scolded me any chance she got. They didn't need to say anything. I sensed that they had secretly disowned me. During a heated exchange between Mama and me, I thought of hurling her pot of onugbu soup against the wall to show her that I couldn't stomach their disdain.

I stomped around the house and acted like I cared very little. I felt hurt. I was somehow comforted that several people regarded me with fear. Of course, not everyone liked me, but I also found it encouraging that my peers treated me as a hero. I was nineteen and eager to collect what the future held.

Besides, I was named after the god of thunder.

## 16.

"Boy, you're playing with fire. You know that?" Uncle Cephas said.

He stood at the window and gazed across the road. It was sunrise, and the delicious aroma of roasted mackerel filled the air. Mama must have sent for him to come and talk sense into my head. If only he could convince my parents of what I was fighting for. Help them to see the bigger picture.

"What's in it for you, Kalu?"

I stared at the wispy beard on his long thin face. He was younger than Mama by five years, but his love for gin made him look much older. He told my parents he was born again, but I occasionally caught him sneaking out of brothels, Bible in hand.

"You've only brought grief to your parents. Look at Jachi. He has bought himself a car," muttered Uncle Cephas. He turned and inspected me. "Have you thought for a second how much you could make from Westoil if you channelled your energies well?"

I wasn't small-minded. Material gains never excited me. Bobo always reminded us that no amount of money equalled the joy one got from serving others. To offer oneself for a just cause was to rise above the flesh.

"Do you understand that you're making history?" Bobo once asked us. "You may not understand. But you're all history makers." His voice had floated out, a slow and gentle lyric, causing my body to tingle all over.

There was a time Bobo spoke about the future of Egbema as though he was reciting a poem. Westoil would annihilate our village, he told us, until not even one ear of grass was left standing. Our villagers would suffer a fate much worse than the acid rains seeping into our pores and scalps—as in Oloibiri's fate. I had never set foot in that deserted town, but people described it as a land of fumes, maggots, and vultures.

I smiled now at the memories of Bobo.

Uncle Cephas flared up, thinking I must have been mocking him.

"Kalu, you think it's funny? Bobo was crazy. He thought this was one big campus where any idiot could kick around with loose ideals. The rest of you have also grown crazy."


## 17.


I ran into Chinwe, my ex-girlfriend, the last week of December. She had been dodging me since we chased Jachi out of our village. She looked like a lean shark, her skin pasty from bleaching cream. Eczema-like spots scattered on her neck, arms, and legs. Her cheekbones stuck out. Jachi had bragged about sleeping with her. It had taken me over four months to even peek at her breasts. She now cried upon seeing me. I shoved her aside and went straight to The Brothers' meeting place.

## 18.

Days later, we were eating breadfruit at Madam Sunshine's.

"Sad, I tell you," an old drunk said, smacking his lips. "Hoodlums have sprung up everywhere, no better than before. The Brothers should be happy now."

The room fell silent as the other drinkers glanced over at us. Everyone knew that the staff's residences at Westoil had been vandalized. Doors stood unhinged, broken. Louvres in pieces. Stuffing ripped from the furniture. Even the Staff Club looked like a bulldozer had torn half of it down. A few boys had carted away electronic gadgets, clothing, and footwear, and some had even started to re-sell the stolen property.

Madam Sunshine strolled in and asked if anyone had called for more beer. When no one responded, she collected empty bottles and plates from the tables and returned to her kitchen. In a minute or so, Tiwa Savage began to sing "Eminado" on the radio in a corner of the kitchen.

"Blame Jachi and his gang," a man said. "They caused all this. Where's the coward, tell me?"

"You've spoken well," said another, clapping for him. "What about his High-mess, Eze? He's only concerned about his throne and the gifts he receives from Westoil."

"Even juju couldn't help Chief Uka," someone else said.

The old drunk watched us for a while, then nodded and murmured, "Tomorrow is pregnant. What will come out of its womb is anybody's guess."

"Old soldier never dies." A lady hailed him from the corner where she sat.

Everybody, even the old drunk, broke out laughing, except for us. We'd heard from a source that Jachi was recruiting boys in a neighbouring village to launch an attack. It didn't bother us, though, since we were fully prepared. More than a dozen boys had sworn to fight on our side.

## 19.

On the way home that evening, we saw two familiar figures strolling out of the barbershop. Members of Jachi's gang. They were chuckling. We glanced at one another. Were they here to spy on us?

"Get them both!" Uzzi yelled.

The two boys looked up and took to their heels. We chased. They ran as fast as deer. We sprinted after them with all our might. The first boy slipped. The others swept by me and swooped in on him. He tried to scuttle away but blows flattened him to the ground.

I tore after the second boy. He leaped over a low barbed-wire fence. I thought I'd lost him, but the wires snagged his leg, and he yowled in pain. We finally got hold of him. I panted so hard my mouth turned dry.

Danny drove his foot into the boy's face as he tried to crawl away. His nose gave a sickening crunch. His cry split the air.

I punched the boy's stomach, knocking him down.

"Stop! Please, stop!" he began screaming. "I can't breathe. I can't breathe."

We didn't care if his heart was going kaput. We simply dragged him like the trash he was to where his partner was squirming on the ground.

"Let's finish them off," Danny said, swinging a steel rod he had found nearby.

Uzzi thought about it and finally grinned. "Undress, you two. Now."

The captives cried for mercy, lifting their hands to him. Sweat poured down faces that were already bruised from several blows and kicks. Uzzi growled, pushing his chest out and balling his fists. The boys winced and bumped into each other.

We decided not to kill them.

That evening, we paraded them naked through the streets.

## 20.

A canopied truck appeared in our village after the Easter celebrations. Twenty fierce-looking uniformed men jumped out of the truck, wielding equally fierce-looking guns. When they arrived that morning in April 2009, every boy in the village had vanished.

## 21.

We made our home in a broken-down sawmill building. It was overgrown with weeds and boarded up with cardboards. Plane trees shaded the mill, their shadows dense and teeming. We felt safe hiding in the forest, where trees grew so tall they loomed like towers. The River Urashi flowed less than two kilometres away. We stayed there for days, barely sleeping. We lived mostly off udara, cashews, and avocadoes. We knew the soldiers were trying to sniff out where we were, but they didn't know the depths of the forest like we did.

On the fifth day, when the moon climbed the sky, we heard a whistle. We stopped talking and flattened ourselves on the floor. Then we heard the crunch of twigs at the door. Our breaths quickened. We exchanged glances.

I thought of running out headlong, but caution held me back.

"It's Oge," someone said.

Uzzi jumped up and peeped through the slats.

We sighed and stepped out. Bobo's sister stood before us with two plastic bags bursting at their seams.

"Who told you we were here?" Uzzi asked her, looking around frantically. We stood alert in case someone had tailed her.

"Bobo and I used to come here to listen to birdsongs," replied Oge.

We glanced at each other. Bobo had also brought us here to think, plan, and dream.

Oge held out the bags and we all gathered around her. She presented us with some akara and bread, tins of sardines and baked beans, sachets of Milo, milk, and water, and bottles of groundnuts. We perched on the grass and started nibbling in silence.

Oge stared at me, then lowered her eyes. I knew that once this madness was over, I would make her my girlfriend. I still longed to hold her in my arms.

"They've killed people," she said. "One mechanic was shot in the head."

I glanced down and balled my fists.

"Those men have set up checkpoints everywhere. They've turned our girls into slaves, passing them around like a soccer ball."

The others were beginning to bristle and seethe.

I close my eyes to stop the anger raging through my body. Far off in the distance, birds cheeped and chirped. I felt an insect creep across my foot, and I flinched. I opened my eyes to see a beetle with luminous yellow wings. I picked it up and watched it twitch its antennae and tiny legs, powerless in my grasp. I squashed it between my fingers, pleased with the crackling sound its shells made.

Before Oge slipped away, she looked at me again, this time a bit longer.

"Your parents..."

I sprang to my feet.

"...are fine," she continued softly. "But the men are harassing them."

Anger turned my tongue into a useless organ. I tried not to imagine what the soldiers were doing to Papa and Mama. But I was powerless, like the beetle I had just crushed to death.


## 22.


Midway, I stopped to catch my breath. I was entering further into the forest, all by myself. Night was closing in on me. Fear cut through my heart. I was lucky to have narrowly escaped the soldiers.

I hadn't prayed for a very long time, but I found myself interlacing my fingers. I could only imagine what Uzzi and the others were going through at the hands of the soldiers. I hoped they hadn't been killed. Or maybe death would be easier than the torture the soldiers probably had in mind. We had planned to leave the village in the dead of night after yesterday's visit from Oge, but it had rained without warning, nonstop. And we'd gotten stranded in the mill.

Then something happened.

On the sixth day, we all woke up late. The sun was already high. The six of us were still holed up in that musty old building.

My stomach had tightened like it was wedged with stone. When I couldn't take it any longer, I burst out, "I need to shit."

They laughed at me, the first laughter in days.

Uzzi joked. "Do you need permission? Shit in my mouth."

I swung my arse in his face. He hissed and shoved me aside. I patted my arse, then ran off giggling into the bush. It had felt good to laugh without feeling stalked after such a long time. I crouched among some cocoyam bushes. The air was delicious and pure, untouched by Westoil's gas flaring.

Then I heard gunshots in the trees and dived to the ground. I held my breath as rushing footsteps and high-pitched voices resounded a few yards away. The sound of something heavy thudded on the ground. I thought of scrambling up and blending in with the chaos, but I couldn't pull my boxers up.

My whole body had gone numb.

"Don't let a single one of them escape," a voice thundered. "Search in and out. Everywhere!"

My teeth started to chatter. I couldn't see anything but black spots until I heard an ear-splitting cry.

"Are you mad? Oh, you want to run away?"

Several images tumbled through my head. The times I disobeyed my parents. The people I made fun of. The girls my friends and I stalked. The shops I pilfered from. The posters of politicians I defaced. The first time I smoked hemp. The images made my eyes sting. I couldn't say how long I stayed on the ground.

Crows cawed overhead.

I felt my palms itch, knowing I wasn't going to see The Brothers ever again.

## 23.

I wondered why I had joined The Brothers in the first place. Maybe I had found it tempting, an adventure. I remembered climbing a hill behind my cousin's house in Jos. It was in 2004, the first time I failed the junior secondary school exams. Mama had sent me off to live with her brother. She hoped I could learn better in a different city.

As I looked out the window every morning, I had imagined what it would feel like to stand on top of that hill. It dared me every time I gazed out. Reached out to me in my dreams. I pictured the hill as a girl I desired to take into my arms, convinced that it wanted to be embraced. One afternoon, I braced myself and climbed it. I couldn't describe exactly how I felt at the time, other than electric. I remembered my mouth was dry as I stood on the peak. I felt like some great explorer, the misty wind against my cheeks. I spread my arms, longing to leap into the air and clap my feet. The fantastic experience taught me to take every difficulty as a hill to be mounted. This climb happened four or five years before the pipeline explosion. Before gangs seeped into our village.

I had to find a way to stay alive right now. I couldn't imagine what kind of nightmare Mama must be going through. I felt sorry for her. She would grieve that her only son had been gunned down somewhere in the forest. Did she know I was sorry? I hoped she would forgive me for being so stubborn. As for Papa, I didn't think he would grieve. I could see him smoking cigarette after cigarette. He had known beforehand how I would turn out, what lay ahead of me. He often reminded me of a fly following a corpse into the grave.

Papa had woken me up one November night, a couple of weeks after Bobo had founded The Brothers. He made me stand by the window and asked me to look at the horizon. I saw nothing spectacular except for the familiar flames scorching the sky.

"You see that gas flare?"

I nodded drowsily.

Papa continued. "Can you hold it with your hands?"

I yawned, then shook my head.

"So, what are you doing to yourself?"

I grumbled in Igbo, *"Aghotaghi m?"*

"What's there not to understand? You're not a child, Kalu. What makes you think you can put out such wild flames?"

I tried to explain. "Somebody has to speak against the mess—"

"Foolishness does not run in our family," Papa cut me off. "Son, let this be the last time I have to speak to you about this. I don't want you to attend any youth meeting again, or I will wash my hands of you."

## 24.

I reached the River Urashi at sunset. I sat down on the bank and tried not to think about The Brothers. The vast pea-green waters shimmered before me. A ladybug landed on my arm. It looked different from the black-spotted red ones I usually saw. This one had a golden shell with black spots. I wanted to squash its tiny body, but I picked it so gently off my arm and dropped it on a dry leaf between my feet. I watched it find its way.

I blew out air and hoped Oge was safe.

Then I closed my eyes and imagined myself in a canoe, gliding toward the point where the sand met the sky.

# RAIN

Dubem stumbled out of bed and pushed away thoughts of his father. He didn't want to recall the peaceful, smiling face that had appeared to him last night. He raced to the washroom and, relieving himself, asked God to help his mother to live longer than his father had lived. Whenever Dubem mentioned her health, she claimed that she was as strong as firewood.

His father had also shown no sign of illness, yet one morning, on his way to the washroom, he'd keeled over, his pants wet with piss and bunched around his knees. Some people said it was heart failure; others said someone had poisoned him. Dubem hadn't known what to believe because he'd been searching for a different job in Lagos when his father collapsed. Dubem worked as a loading assistant in a Lebanese-owned company on Mile 2 until the government shut it down for churning out adulterated fruit juice. Unable to find a job for over one year, he had scurried back to Amuzi, his village in Imo State.

After the washroom, Dubem trudged back to his room, wishing the neighbourhood didn't whisper about him. He found it difficult to ignore the mothers who scrunched their noses at him, the fathers who threw him thinly veiled stares laced with pity and disappointment. Even when he wasn't around them, he could hear their voices:

"That one, he wasted his life in the city and came back, empty- handed, to be breastfed by his mother."

"*Odiegwu*. He'll break his mother's heart. Just like his father. The men in that family are useless."

"You call them men? Lazybones. Only good enough to be kicked in the yansh."

Dubem gazed out the window and frowned. There was no trace of the sun, only the looming shadows of rain. A thread of smoke climbed into the sky. Who could be burning bush in July when the farming season had passed? He prayed it wouldn't rain. He prayed his appointment with Cheta would turn out well. His childhood friend had just returned to Nigeria after eight years abroad and had promised Dubem that he'd help him move to Malaysia, where young men had mastered the art of fleecing rich white widows.

As Dubem turned away from the window, he spotted her—the neighbour girl he had been admiring since he got back to his hometown some five months ago. She lived with her parents in a double- storey building, two houses away. He watched her glide by, a black handbag swinging from her shoulder. He held off the urge to call out her name, the one that he'd heard her parents scream. He pictured himself buying her shimmering items. He liked anything silver. Would she want something better than that? Gold, maybe?

Dubem always got a hard-on when he fantasized about women, but with her, things were different, which he figured was a good sign. He had once watched a film about a man who, for years, was secretly in love with a lady. The evening he decided to approach her, he found out that she had moved away. He never got the chance to tell her how he felt.

Dubem ducked from the window when the girl glanced in his direction. Once, she had caught him staring at her, and she had smiled, showing dimpled cheeks, brown lips, and cream-coloured teeth. He found himself tongue-tied each time she smiled. He had never spoken more than the same three words—*How are you?*—to her, even though they locked eyes, fleetingly, every time their paths crossed.

Something knotted in his chest, and he worried that she had heard the rumours about him from the villagers. Did she also think little of him like the other villagers did?

Dubem continued to peep at her until she swept down the street toward the main road. He put on a black T-shirt, slid his cellphone into his pocket, and stuffed in a few notes he had taken from his mother's purse. He headed for the door, hoping there would be no rain.

*

Outside, his mother sat under a rusty tin roof bolstered by wooden poles half-mauled by termites. Her fingers were white from the bean paste she was moulding. Dubem watched her dunk each ball into the pan of boiling oil. They sizzled and hissed, turning from white to golden in a blink.

"Ma, good morning." He fanned the motes of ash from his face.

His mother raised her head, squinting through the fumes at him. Her face had blackened from the firewood smoke. "Have you eaten?" she asked. "I left some akara and bread in the cupboard."

Dubem wanted to tell her about his dream, how his father had held out his hands to him, smiling more peacefully than ever. But the smile, rather than reassuring Dubem, had gnawed his heart. He wasn't superstitious at all, but the dream disturbed him. He still felt terrible that he contributed nothing to his father's burial. He longed to talk to his mother about his frustration, but it would be like turning on a tap that no one could ever shut again. She would go on and on about restless ghosts, evil relatives, and envious neighbours.

"I'm going to see Cheta," Dubem said instead. "I'll eat when I come back."

"Ha, Cheta? That boy." She sucked her teeth. "Where does he get all that money from?" She turned the bean cakes over with a ladle.

"Do you want me to ask him for you?"

Like Dubem, Cheta was an only child, but people said that he was worth more than four children put together. Some parents held him up as a model. They wanted their children to become as rich as Cheta was because he donated bags of rice and beans to widows and handed out bundles of naira to the elders in his clan anytime he visited Nigeria.

"*Mba nu.* Have you seen the house he built for his father? The car he bought for his mother? People say he's into, well, only God knows."

"Into what, Ma?"

She reproached him with a frown as though she found him insulting.

Dubem studied her pinched, longsuffering face and felt his shoulders droop. He shifted his gaze to the sieve dripping with oil. There were times he worried he wouldn't have enough to foot her bills if she ended up in the hospital. What could be more disgraceful to any parent than a son who couldn't pay for his own mother's coffin? Dubem had failed to contribute even one naira to his father's burial. He was sure people mocked him for that.

"But is it true?"

"True what?"

"What people say about him. *Ogwu ego.* That he sold his kidney, made money out of it," she said. "He is not a politician. How else could he have come by so much money?"

Dubem knew better than to argue with her because she often clung to her opinion, tighter than a dictator clung to power. Still, with a tic of irritation, he shook his head and said, "How will you enjoy your wealth if you have only one kidney? Ma, stop listening to people!"

"I don't listen to them. They come here and tell me stories."

Dubem disliked how the villagers badmouthed each other like they had nothing better to do. They would praise him before his mother, then speak ill of him behind her back. Small-minded midgets. He hated living in Amuzi where nothing thrived but weeds and ill will. It was only a matter of time before he would chance upon piles of money and soften his mother's careworn face.

"See you later, Ma."

"You be careful with that Cheta boy."

Her dark tone sent a chill down his spine. She sounded like Cheta was going to pawn his kidney. For a fleeting second, Dubem caught a glimpse of himself curled up at a smelly shrine in the middle of a forest—his mouth gagged, his hands and feet bound, his skin blistered—being used for a money ritual.

He shook his head at this dark image and told his mother to be careful with the hot oil.

*

Dubem turned a street corner and almost bumped into a shabby old man walking dazedly in circles. He wanted to apologize but heard him mumbling to himself. Dubem suspected he had lost his mind, so he said nothing and quickened his pace. As he raised his head, he saw two girls approaching. He recognized them because they lived with their parents on the opposite street.

The girls noticed Dubem, darted glances at each other, then spoke in a whisper. They wiggled their hips as they drew nearer. The taller girl wore ripped jeans, while her friend flaunted a red halter top. He winked at them and parted his lips in a smile. They shrank away when he tried to reach out a hand to them.

"Fine girls," Dubem said, grinning. "Where are you going?"

"None of your business."

He stopped walking. "You don't want to visit with me?"

"Visit you, *kwa*?" scoffed the taller one. "We've heard about you."

"You can't even buy a bottle of malt and a meat pie," her friend chipped in.

Dubem brushed their taunts aside, offering a wider smile. "I'll take you to Shoprite, and you can buy all the peppered chicken and meat pies you want."

The girls whispered to each other. They giggled, their palms over their mouths.

"Your mates are buying girls the latest phones, and you're bragging about snacks. Might as well offer us a pan of akara," the taller girl said, hooking an arm around her friend's waist.

They strutted off, their backsides jiggling.

Dubem chafed at the mention of akara as though they had insulted his mother. The girls had mouths like razors. He was sure they would buzz around him like mosquitoes if he returned to the village with wads of cash. He hurried along, dodging the potholes mottled with murky water and litter. He smiled at the clouds that had softened to splashes of blue and white. The sun still lurked somewhere unseen in the sky. He was convinced it would not rain.

Dubem waved and nodded at the people in the stalls that mushroomed along his street, then stopped at a kiosk packed with beverages, confectionaries, and condiments to buy a sachet of rum. At the bus stop, he peered at his wrist. He remembered that he had pawned his expensive silver watch for a measly one thousand naira—just like he had pawned his Nike sneakers and suede wallet for less than three thousand naira. This time, he was willing to wager his life for something more durable. Something of value for himself and his mother.

Cheta would teach him how to walk tall. He was always dependable, come rain come shine. Dubem smiled and brought out the sachet of rum. He tore the tip open with his teeth and swigged the sweetish amber contents whole. A soft flame caressed his throat.

The snarl of commuters pressed Dubem from all sides while he waited for a taxi to town. He pulled the naira notes out of his pocket to check that none were missing, smoothed them out, and counted three hundred and seventy naira. It was all he had on him, but it was enough to get him into town, plus buy two bottles of stout.

Some noisy boys argued on the other side of the road. They were arguing about soccer and winnings in front of a girl in a green shirt seated behind a desk under a green lotto umbrella. That was where Dubem had gambled away the money he'd made from pawning his prized items; money he would have used to buy foodstuffs for his mother. After that loss, he vowed to never step foot in the betting centre again.

Maybe, though, he should try his luck one last time.

*

"Shit!" Dubem muttered, standing before the pillared, wrought-iron gate of a massive house. He had waited over an hour to get a taxi to this place, only to be told by the uniformed guard that Cheta wasn't home. But Cheta had assured him two days ago that he would be in all day.

The guard scrutinized him through the peephole.

Dubem raised his hand as if for emphasis. "Please, I am his best *friend*. He's meant to see me this morning."

"*Ngwanu*. Call am for phone," the guard responded, as though he would rather be elsewhere sipping ogogoro.

Dubem got an annoying busy tone when he dialled Cheta's number. He tried again, but the line was still busy. He tried once more, then gave up. He scratched the back of his neck. Cheta had forgotten about their meeting. Or was he avoiding him?

He redialled the number, and a voice droned, telling him to call back later.

"Na network," the guard suggested.

Dubem didn't think so. "Is there somewhere I could sit down and wait?"

The guard shook his head.

Dubem looked around himself. "No bench anywhere?"

"Na there," the guard pointed to a guava tree close to the gate, "people dey wait if dey wan see Chief."

Chief? Dubem lifted his brow. When did his friend get that title? Even though Cheta was just thirty, three years Dubem's junior, he owned several luxury cars, including a Lincoln Navigator and a G-Benz. He also owned an imposing home adorned with pilasters, cornices, figurines, and glass bay windows. Perhaps one could even address him as *onye eze*—the king.

Dubem leaned against the guava tree, which was barely leafy enough to offer shade. The air around him seethed with heat. Sweat dribbled down his face. He mopped his brow with his hand. His body itched, and his hairy armpits were sticky. He grew frustrated and chided himself for wearing black.

The sun, which had been missing since dawn, now glared in the centre of the sky. It seared hot like it wanted to make up for its belatedness. Dubem wished the clouds would darken. The wind soon unfurled and tossed dry leaves across his path. It offered only a slight coolness to his arms but not enough to stop him from sweating.

What could be more fucked up than this? Dubem slapped his palm against his wet forehead. How could Cheta treat him with such disregard? The phone line remained busy. Had his friend travelled back to Malaysia? Dubem knew that scammers kept their schedule a secret. They stole into the country like phantoms and disappeared just as stealthily.

The air turned hazy for a moment. Dubem tried to relax, but his throat was parched. Hunger made him feel a little wobbly, and he regretted not eating breakfast. He suddenly yearned for another nip of rum to soothe his nerves. He left the shade and rapped his knuckles on the gate.

The guard flashed an eye through the peephole. "What is it now?"

"Iced water. Please?"

Dubem didn't complain when the guard handed him a glass of lukewarm water instead. He drank it and asked for more. He finally felt revived.

"What's the time now?"

The guard scowled at him. "I no get watch."

Dubem scowled back. "Idiot," he hissed under his breath before stomping off.

*

Dubem swore at himself when he realized that he had taken the wrong exit. Commercial motorcycles and tricycles did not operate in this part of New Owerri. Many of the mansions there belonged to politicians, who believed that safety and prestige meant banning public transportation from entering their neighbourhood. He swore again because he would have to trek all the way to Concorde Hotel to get to the bus stop.

The sun glowered. The air seemed to crackle—or was it his shirt? Dubem warded off anger as he skulked his way out of the elite neighbourhood. Dogs barked behind gates spiked with barbed wire. His knees ached, and he was tired. He already had covered a fair distance by the time an engine rumbled nearby. He saw it was an okada dropping a passenger off at the IBC gate.

Just as Dubem cupped his hands to call out to the motorcyclist, he heard a honk behind him and jumped to the sidewalk. He hadn't even realized that he had strayed onto the road.

"Dubem-Silver!"

He recognized the tinny voice. It felt like a damp towel on his hot skin. Only Cheta called him that. Dubem spun round.

A red GMC Yukon pulled up next to him.

"Dude, how far?" Cheta called out from the back window.

Dubem hid his surprise. His friend had a goatee. His hair was slick and dyed blond.

"Get in." Cheta gestured to the other passenger door.

Dubem sat next to him in the backseat. He nodded to the smooth-shaven driver who wore a gold stud in his left ear. He and Cheta gave each other playful jabs, like long-lost friends reunited.

Oritsefemi sang jauntily about Malaysia and Miami on the car stereo.

The chilly breeze from the vents soothed Dubem. He saw himself in the rear-view mirror and flushed at the sight of his sweat-stained clothes. He regretted not having had his bath and hoped the perfumed air in the car would mask his body odour.

Cheta looked him up and down. "Boy, you ne'er fuckin' change ooo," he said, bobbing his head and shoulders to Orit-sefemi's gusty song.

Dubem couldn't get over the way his friend glowed. Cheta wore a simple purple V-neck, with "Get Rich or Die Trying" inscribed on the front.

"*If I like,*" Cheta sang, weaving his hands back and forth, "*I spend my money any way I like.*"

"Hustle your money, guy," Dubem gushed. "See you, you done fat up like hippopotamus. Wetin you dey chop sef?" He almost touched his friend's skin, smooth as a mackerel's.

"Boy, na fiscal."

"*Biko,* which one be fiscal?"

Cheta cuffed him on the back of his head, chuckling. "This village done fuck up your oblongata. Fiscal, our slang for money."

Dubem rolled the word "fiscal" over his tongue. It tasted heavy and forceful. He eyed the coral beads on his friend's wrists, the gold chains around the neck. Envy needled his chest.

"You be Chief, ehn?" he asked.

"Those who are Chiefs, how many fuckin' heads dem get?" said Cheta. "Dude, nothing dey inside these things, all is fiscal. I put on weight is because I eat fiscal and drink fiscal. In short, guys for Malaysia dey call me Fuck Fiscal. You fit call me Che Malaysia. I don use Queen Elizabeth's face clean my yansh.

I piss on dollars. I smoke white with euros. Even woo-woo. Money is fuckin' honey. Boy, any person who tell you say money no good, fuck dat person's papa till kingdom come!"

"You smoke white? Which one be woo-woo?"

"Big C."

"Guy, all these names wetin dem mean?"

"Cocaine. Boy, you be old school."

Dubem regarded him with both fascination and bafflement. His friend reminded him of American hip-hop celebrities with their frivolous lifestyle. Is this what surplus money did to people? A once timorous and taciturn boy now spoke in a twang of expletives, as though he could smack anybody in the face and not care about it. This couldn't be his friend talking.

"Guy, you come keep me waiting for hours," Dubem grumbled.

Cheta didn't apologize. Instead, he eyeballed Dubem. "You dey vex?"

Dubem was angry, but he also desperately needed his friend's help, so he shook his head.

"Guys go hustle." Cheta started describing Malaysia— beaches, bikinis, beer, barbecues. A land where nobody slaved nor starved. People had shindigs from Thursdays to Sundays. The way Cheta explained it, Dubem pictured a country belching cash into the laps of foreigners. He couldn't wait to leave this godforsaken Nigeria. His skin would glisten when he returned home after spending a few years abroad. Girls would ogle him and long to touch his arms. He was already more attractive than Cheta, after all.

"You remember as girls dey yab us like lepers?" Cheta's upper lip slanted as he thumped his chest. "Now, I be their daddy. I organize girls to dance Mapouka naked. Anytime. All is fiscal. Call me Che Malaysia."

Dubem considered telling Cheta about the two girls who had insulted him on his way that morning, but his friend continued to talk about nude parties, which distracted Dubem with its glamour.

"Ehen," Cheta exclaimed. "You heard police caught Thunder Bay?"

Dubem shook his head. He hadn't checked his Facebook or Instagram for a long time because he couldn't pay for enough airtime on his cellphone, so there was no way he could have heard about Thunder Bay's arrest. But then, he had known that fate would deal an uppercut to the extravagant multi-millionaire fraudster. The Nigerian Canadian was known for cloning credit cards and showing off his riches on Instagram. Thunder Bay owned a collection of fedoras, trench coats, crocodile leather shoes, gold wristwatches, champagne, and cars. He sprayed dollars, flaunting everything down to his CK underwear. Thunder Bay organized parties for the heirs of African presidents and splashed champagne down the cleavages of girls of different sizes and colours. Scantily dressed white girls posed with him on his yacht in the middle of a shiny blue sea. Some of the girls had their arms thrown in the air and were laughing like there was no hunger in the world. It was the photos of those girls that stung Dubem's heart.

"How possible? Where him dey when police catch am?" he asked.

Cheta stroked the arm of his leather seat. "For him base in Canada nah. Why police no go catch am? Spending money anyhow and posing up and down for Instagram. Like say na him father be the Prime Minister. Guy, no be all oyibo be mugu o."

Dubem gave a little shiver of glee. Everyone seemed to adore Thunder Bay, though he made Nigerians back home feel as if they had mush for brains. He also made Dubem sad, furious, and envious all at the same time. People would now laugh at Thunder Bay, at his life behind bars.

"He acted like nobody could touch him," Dubem said.

"Police catch him guys too, all of dem—Pablo, Big Egbon, Glow Master, Bespoke, Lord Dubai. Chai, God no go let those guys spoil market for everybody," Cheta hissed, leaned forward, and popped open a small cabinet containing a cooler.

"This is Perrier-Jouét!" he announced as if in triumph, holding up a corked bottle. "Guess how much?"

Dubem simply tossed a figure into the air.

"Booooy, you insult me," Cheta groaned. He tilted the bottle toward Dubem. "Do I look like a person who drinks fuckin' zobo? This is 70k." He mentioned the amount off-handedly like it was nothing.

Dubem gaped at his friend in disbelief. Madness. His mother, who sat frying akara every day through the month, had never once in her life made that sum. How could anyone who'd grown up poor waste such money on a drink? Something you would pee out in a few hours. It wasn't even a carton of champagne, just a single bottle. But he didn't want to be denied his friend's charity, so he kept quiet.

Cheta handed him a glass frothing with bubbles. "How's your old woman?"

"She just dey struggle." Dubem held the glass delicately as if it could slip out of his hand at any moment. He was afraid to even take a sip.

"Nothing like a mother. Come, let's chop money while we're young." Cheta smiled and clinked his glass against Dubem's.

They both drank at the same time. The wine tasted like coconut milk and vanilla. Dubem longed to close his eyes, to fill his senses with its sweetness. He had never tasted such a flavour before. This was how life was meant to be, smooth, full of richness. He thought of the neighbour girl and imagined them sipping the expensive alcohol together.

"So, dude." Cheta leaned sideways, sizing Dubem up. "What's up with your fuckin' life?" he asked.

*

Dubem paused on the road, off the muddy patch, where motorcyclists hovered like vultures. Cheta had ordered his driver to "offload" him at that section of the estate. Dubem could hardly believe his good luck. He had to bite his finger to make sure he wasn't dreaming. He would not have gotten what he'd earned just now if he had worked for six months. A block of crisp one-hundred-naira notes pressed against his thigh. Cheta had dropped ten of it into his palm without so much as moving an eyelash. None of the people Dubem knew, affluent or otherwise, had shown him such generosity. Though he wished that his friend had given him some more.

"Call me Dubem-Fuckin'-Silver," Dubem said with a chuckle.

He straightened his shoulders and walked proud and confident. He had almost lost all hope until Cheta reappeared and promised to lift him up—"open his eyes" to making "fast money." Dubem would no longer have to travel to Malaysia. Cheta had suggested he remain in Owerri and manage the "local internet runs" with some of his boys, who operated out of an ordinary-looking but well-furnished bungalow somewhere in the rich neighbourhood of Works Layout. Cheta would buy him a laptop with a modem after he got back from his trip to Abuja, which would be in a week. Dubem wondered what he would do with himself in the meantime.

A bounce appeared in his steps as he headed toward the clique of motorcyclists. Good things rarely happened to him, and he hoped he would be lucky from now on. Dubem considered what to buy for his mother. He also considered what he would get for the neighbour girl. He'd make her his wife. She had to fall for him now, while it was authentic. Before dollars started pouring out of his pockets, and he attracted the attention of other girls.

Dubem clambered onto an okada. "Douglas Market," he instructed the motorcyclist.

A few minutes later, Dubem climbed down from the okada when they got to the bus stop opposite Ama Hausa, a mini bazaar where people exchanged their foreign currencies. The dust and heat in the air filled his nostrils. Pedestrians bustled through the street and jostled each other. Drivers fumed and honked as they manoeuvred their vehicles through the jam-packed road. The din of traders and hagglers drummed in a frenzy all around him.

Dubem picked out a jewel shop next to St. Paul's Anglican Church. The moment he entered the poorly lit shop, the elderly owner appraised him with swift, beady eyes. Dubem felt unsettled, as though the eyes would drop to the floor if they moved too fast. He greeted the jeweller and scanned the variety of jewels in the display cases. He pointed at a silver necklace with a red heart pendant. The jeweller slipped a bunch of keys out of his pocket, opened the case, and handed him the necklace.

"I don't sell fakes," the jeweller said when Dubem asked if it was genuine.

"How much?"

"Five thousand."

"Five—what?" Dubem gasped.

"It's silver," replied the jeweller.

"So what? How much be gold, then?"

Dubem suspected the jeweller might be seeing double from the way his eyes rolled this way and that. Did the light in the shop bother his eyes? Dubem mulled over the amount. What if the neighbour girl rejected him after he got her such a costly gift?

The gems around the shop glittered, tempting him. A thought started to flower in his mind, but he pushed it away.

The jeweller hoisted himself onto the stool by his glass counter. He looked gruff, like he had no time to entertain indecision. He cleared his throat and muttered, "Please, if you don't want to buy anything, then kindly leave my shop. I don't want bad market."

Dubem considered him a bully and dipped a hand into his pocket. He would pay for the silver necklace. Out of the corner of his eye, a shadow darted behind him. Dubem swung around.

He had only enough time to catch a glimpse of a black T-shirt blending into a nearby shop full of mannequins in clingy shirts and stem-thin pants. Was he being trailed? Afraid that he could lose his money, he patted his side pockets to make sure it was intact.

"Let me have the necklace," Dubem demanded. "If it ever fades, I will make sure to bring trouble to your doorstep."

The jeweller rolled his eyes again and slid the necklace into a little white box. He then handed it to Dubem, who paid for it and slipped it into his pocket. He imagined the neighbour girl in his arms, spilling tears of joy over the necklace. Thinking of her, he felt like leaping into the air and kicking his feet together. He could sprint down the road like a madman, but he restrained himself.

"Damn! Is this what it feels like to have your manhood again?" he said under his breath. "A man without money is a man without an erection. There's a kind of music only those who are rich can hear. That music is not for church rats." He laughed out loud because those were the words his father used to say.

The jeweller shot him a look of surprise.

Dubem masked his excitement and walked out of the shop. He stood under the awning of the building, but only long enough to feel the dusty breeze against his cheeks. He smiled at the simmering blue sky. The sunlight coursed through his body.

Let it rain and flood the city!

He couldn't care right now.

Still though, he deliberated whether to board a bus or a tricycle. The idea of chartering a taxi and having the entire backseat to himself tickled his groin. But, no, he wasn't going to squander his money just yet. He'd never gamble away his money again because he had to think about his loved ones. He was going to make his mother proud, her life better.

Dubem had walked only a few paces when he stopped on the sidewalk to fish out the precious item from his pocket. He felt like a little boy who couldn't wait to unwrap his Christmas present. He had been flat broke for too long and was eager to shake off the raw shame that tormented and often prevented him from going for a walk around the neighbourhood. He knew his neighbours secretly ridiculed him. He looked forward to seeing their faces now that he had recovered his manhood.

It felt so fantastic to be whole again!

As Dubem opened the box and admired the silver necklace, an incredibly balmy feeling overtook him. He'd never been able to afford such an object before. Now, he could pay for ten of such necklaces and still have enough money left in his pockets. He liked that the necklace had a heart and that it was red.

"Love is written in blood," he mused, smiling to himself.

A rare gift for the girl he loved. He was eager to see her expression when she held the shimmering present in her palm. He knew his mother would approve of her. But, maybe, he should give the jewel to his mother instead. He hadn't bought her any presents for over five years now. He could always get the girl something else or buy her any clothes of her choice.

Pleased with his decision, Dubem started to slip the box back into his side pocket, but someone shoved him in the shoulder. He struggled to catch himself from falling as the figure streaked past him. Dubem crumpled on the sidewalk, catching sight of a glittery object in the man's hands. He recognized the black T-shirt.

Dubem shuddered in alarm as the owner of the jewellery shop cried, "Thief, thief, thief!" His voice knifed through the humid air. Dubem scrambled to his feet, cradling his injured shoulder. He had let go of the box. He began to frantically look around for it.

There!

Only a few paces ahead.

He reached to grab it, but a crowd had surged from nowhere to surround him. Someone kicked the box out of his reach.

The chorus of *thief, thief, thief* roared in his ears. A squall of voices.

Dubem's heart scuttled around his chest. He fumbled around for the box.

"Wey the thief?"

"He ran that way!"

"No, he ran the other way."

"Over there! See am, see am."

"No, no! No be am."

"Na him! Look am, look am!" A boy pointed down at him.

Dubem spotted the little white box a few feet away. He froze. Then he panicked. He was being mistaken for the thief. He leaped toward the box and tried to snatch it off the ground, but the veins in his neck snapped as a shoe landed flat on his hand, grinding it into the dirt. He clenched his teeth, though a howl still slipped through his lips.

Dubem tried to pull his hand free. Another shoed foot caught him in the jaw to launch him even further from the box. The crowd swarmed around and attacked him like a clan of hyenas. He attempted to get to his feet, but a battering of blows and kicks kept him down.

People threw tires at him. A stone struck his head. Scraps of rubbish smacked against his skin.

"But that's not him."

Dubem, stiff with pain, picked out the old jeweller amidst the crowd. His voice sounded as horrified as his face looked. The jeweller continued to protest, but the clamour drowned out his lone voice. Dubem's head buzzed, and he saw the crowd multiplying, their shadows blocking out the sun. Dappled figures appeared to swipe at his face, and he found himself recoiling and sinking into darkness.

Then, suddenly, Dubem saw his father hovering next to the jeweller. He still had that peaceful smile on his wrinkled face, the same one from the dream, and he was sticking out his hand again. Dubem stretched himself to take his father's offer, but someone kicked him in the shoulder. The kick slashed him, swinging him around; all he could do was groan.

At last, with what was left of his strength, Dubem pulled himself up one more time. Like a cornered animal blind and crazed, he rammed headlong into the rumbling crowd. A barrage of metal and wood pushed him back.

Dubem could hear bones crunching.

His bones.

"I say that's not him!"

Dubem could faintly hear the jeweller's final protest drowned by a cacophony of voices. He flailed and flopped down. Someone yanked at his belt, loosening it fast from his waist and his pants slid down his hips. Dubem curled up on his side, remembering how, as a child, he and some boys had clobbered a snake to a bloodied mess.

Through the blur, Dubem saw the tiny white box crushed under the flurry of feet. Fuzzy images of a girl sobbing in his mother's arms flashed across his eyes. He squinted to see a man raising a gallon over his body. Dubem did not see someone strike a match, but he heard the scratchy sound. Gasoline splashed over him, coursing down his cheeks. Its reek, like that of his blood, stung his eyes and nostrils.

Dubem wished now that the heavens would split. He wished, more than ever, for the rain.

*

*(In memory of Tekene, Chiadika,
Toku and Ugonna, October 5, 2012)*

# STUPID

They called an emergency meeting to discuss my situation. I huff quietly to myself, *Lekwa anya!* You'd think I had bashed someone's head against the wall or broken into a store down the street. We are in my cousin's living room, which is twice the size of my parents' shabby bedroom. The rugs are pink-beige, and butterflies soar on the lime green curtains. But they never really fly since they're forever entrapped in the fabric. I used to see myself as trapped, but not anymore. I could soar very high with just the right amount of push.

Currently, I sit on a couch by the door with six family members sitting in a semi-circle around me. They look eager to pass judgement on me. I wish I'd been left out of their meeting. I try not to look anyone in the eye. Not my cousin Nonso, not even his wife, Lebechi. I only told them about my decision to leave their home two weeks ago, after Brother Tobiah assured me that I had his support. I remember how unsettled they had been when I first mentioned it to them.

I'm sure my parents will no longer look upon me as their redeemer. They might have branded me an outcast already. I understand why everybody is angry with me. I do, but I'm only eighteen and they make it seem like I am older. They have lost faith in me. But it's useless crying over broken eggs—or eggs that have already hatched.

They don't know about divine intervention. It's amazing how God can always turn any life around because He already did before. Though I'm not ready for all this drama, I must sit through it and play my part. Brother Tobiah has been pushing me in the right direction since we grew closer than friends. Still, from what I can see now, I fear it's going to be a long day of yapping among family members. That's what family is for, after all.

Talk, talk, talk.

Mama, meanwhile, is teetering on the edge of her seat. She certainly can't wait to wring my neck the minute the tribunal is over. She looks thinner than when I last saw her. I worry that she's too thin, though I say nothing. She is the first to slice the silence, always touchy, always itching to yap away. She shoots a finger at me like a trigger-happy police officer. Luckily, I'm sitting four chairs away from her, so I avoid looking her way.

"You're no different from Didi and your mates," she says.

Suddenly, I'm reminded of girls whose stupidity people still talk about in our village, even after several years. Didi had run away with a loafer to Malawi. A woman stripped Onyeka naked in a fight over her husband. Some drunks left Njideka walking limp after forcing themselves on her at a party. A roadside quack doctor toyed with Oluchi's womb, and she bled to death. All of them teenagers, who got themselves misled by miscreants.

But I'm not anything like them.

"Don't you know how lucky you are?" Papa pipes up, scratching his scraggly goatee. "How many girls have relatives who are willing to help them? It seems you've only grown fat and foolish. Too much food has turned your head."

I look past him. If you had made good of your own life, I wouldn't be here slaving away for your brother's family.

"Uncle, easy. It is okay," my cousin intervenes.

A technician, or electrician—I haven't cared enough to find out what Nonso does for a living. All I can say is that he works for a big company in the Industrial Layout and usually returns home with odd scraps, fiddling with them till he's completely worn out. At this very moment, he is looking more frustrated than let down. Frustrated because his job hardly gives him any breathing space. Frustrated that, from now on, he will have to babysit his twins himself. He is just as busy as his wife. So that's a prospect neither of them is excited about.

If my cousin had his way, he would avoid spending more than a few hours with his boys. They can drive anybody but me crazy. It's only the two of them, six-year-olds, but you'd think a commotion had overtaken the apartment once they started their games. They like to race up and down the living room or kitchen; sometimes, they throw pillows at each other and drum on the table. Other times, they howl and shriek just for the fun of it. There was a time they jumped so hard on the floor that the neighbour living downstairs came stomping up to knock on our door. I could have long ago gone crazy myself, but ever since I learned how to cane them nice and square on the butt without their parents finding out, they now have the sense to act up only when their parents are around.

I long to bite the fresh garden eggs from the tray on the centre table, but everyone seems to be avoiding them. The air is too tense to eat. The bottles of malt and other non-alcoholic drinks remain capped. None of us in the room have made any attempt to move. Not even Papa, who begins each day with a shot of paraga and a stick of cigarette. I'm surprised that he doesn't reek of cigarette fumes. He's probably going to smoke more than a pack by the time this whole meeting is over.

"Look at her eyes," Mama says. Her face is pulled so tight it might snap. "There is no shame in them. I can't believe you have no brain!"

I want to smile at this image of her face, at my brilliance. Brother Tobiah always tells me I have a beautiful imagination.

"Eyes like a she-goat," Papa jokes, trying to lighten the mood, but no one laughs. No one. "You're lucky," he adds. "If you were back in the village, I'd have branded you with a hot knife until you saw the devil himself."

Although I have long stopped caring about what Papa thinks of me, I still feel pity for him. His face is warped like a piece of wood. You'd think he was much older than fifty-five. At times, what vexes me is that he's proud enough to flaunt his tattered life as an example of what it means to be living after he'd blown his chance at leading a much better life. He could have been living comfortably in the city because his elder brother had tried so hard in the past to help him become somebody. But what did Papa do? He wasted the best part of his life in pubs and brothels in Aba, while his mates got busy at school and got themselves careers.

"Eunice, you've dashed every hope of becoming somebody eee," my uncle says. Whenever he speaks, his voice runs with an echo. Maybe because he is round from head to toe. Chief Dr. Zumba has an overhanging belly that's bigger than two pillows squashed together. He is a Chief and Doctor and Knight, a man of titles, so it's easy for him to think everybody must be somebody like he is. Like his two children.

His wife's face is too polished for my liking, and the powder on it could smear two white napkins beige. Lolo Zumba is prettier and far younger than Mama, but she has more bags under her eyes—eye-bags that could be the result of the defeats her husband had suffered in politics.

I want to yawn, but I remind myself to behave. Don't want to disrespect any of them. Be yourself, Brother Tobiah once told me. Status does not count for anything in the sight of God.

"You could have been somebody eee," my uncle goes on, nodding his head, which is twice as large as Papa's. "A graduate. A tailor, at worst. Somebody."

I flick him a glance as if he were a fly. I don't have to be somebody; I hold myself back from snickering. You think you're all smart? How many of our First Ladies have gone to university, if education was that important? I remember a man on the radio who had scoffed at the ex-governor's wife (or was it his mother?) because she'd never seen the four walls of a university campus. Even the last president's wife was unknown—a nobody—until her husband took over the government and she became a celebrity.

"You've brought shame upon yourself, Eunice," Mama says, grabbing a throw pillow but not throwing it at me. "Not me."

I can hear Grandma's flinty voice in hers. Grandma had been a secondary school teacher, and two out of her three daughters had died in their teens. She had dreamt big for them and had hoped her only surviving daughter would pursue at least one of those dreams. But when Grandma found that Mama had allowed a trailer driver, Papa, to make her give up her studies for a life of farming, her heart had flipped and then failed.

It's bitterness, not poverty, I realize, that is eating Mama dry. I'm not making the same mistake. I plan to not live with any regrets.

They look like a sketch of a woebegone family whose collective aspiration has come apart at the seams. They can bemoan my fate—or whatever. Or even accuse me of shitting on our family name. What do I care about inheritance? I'm shocked that none of them thought I desired something different from what they had planned for me. They all assumed that I'd fit into their dream like I have no life of my own.

Papa stands and looks around like he's confused or lost. "The washroom?" he asks.

Nonso points toward the kitchen. "It is on your right, the next door."

Lebechi jumps to her feet and casts her husband a sidelong glance. "Uncle, please come with me. Let me show you the washroom." She gestures for Papa to follow, and Papa smiles at her, showing his teeth the colour of tobacco.

"Thanks, my daughter," he says, trailing behind Lebechi.

I gaze at the floor and realize that I need to paint my toenails. I must look more beautiful for Brother Tobiah, even though he already calls me his cedar of Lebanon. I enjoy hearing him read the Song of Solomon in low, dreamy tones. He often whispers to me that I smell as fragrant as spices plucked from the waters of Euphrates, that my eyes are the shiny beads on his mother's necklace. My heart flutters whenever he says that my love is more potent than wine, that he usually gets as drunk as a sinner from staring at my fat, curvy lips. If it weren't for his fear of God, he said one time, he would shuffle down the street singing Hosanna to my beauty.

I smile a little wistfully, letting my gaze wander to the window.

Outside, the street grows loud and raucous. A hundred or more voices haggle, vehicle horns blare, loudspeakers scream out songs, and generators rattle the evening air. I can pick out strains of Burna Boy's "Another Story" climbing in through the window. My cousin's favourite song. I've never really understood Nonso. He and his wife have more money than my parents could ever make in their lifetimes, but they live in a neighbourhood with kiosks on every corner.

I see Lebechi slipping into the kitchen. She would rather hide in her bedroom fixing her lashes than hang around listening to a bunch of older people. I notice that she is washing something in the sink.

Papa returns to the living room, carelessly fumbling with his zipper. I wince at this sight and glance away, praying he does not make an excellent fool of himself. Mama also catches him; she eyeballs him and murmurs something under her breath, which I know is anything but flattering. Papa seems not to care about his clumsiness. He slouches next to Mama on the couch, throws his legs wide apart like he owns the apartment, and smiles at her, barely showing any teeth.

My uncle is saying something about the children of today. He breaks off as his daughter-in-law struts into the living room, her shoulders level like a ruler. Lebechi always reminds me of one of those skinny girls on TV. She pretends not to be a snob,

although I occasionally see her turning up her nose as if everything around her stinks. She sits next to her husband, pressing
her lips into a thin line. She starts filing her long nails.

I wonder why she wears those fake things. Like her husband,
she thinks I can't figure out what I want for the rest of my life.
She believed I was going to be around much longer than my
elder sister had been with our cousin's family. Abigail had
looked after four children, two of whom are now in university.
Yet what does she have to show for the sixteen years she spent
living with our cousin's family? Nothing! *Uwa nka le.* Abigail is in
her mid-forties and miserable. Men ask her for sex, and that's
all they want from her. Everyone says that she has passed her
prime and will never get married.

As for me, I will not allow anyone to use and discard me
like trash. It's only a stupid person who will continue wasting
herself on other people's dreams.

The sudden silence in the room gnaws on me—anything
but silence. Anything. I want to lean over and grab a bottle of
malt. Then, leaning back in my seat, I would let go of the bottle
and watch it shatter into a million pieces all over the carpeted
floor. The action would throw my family into pure rage. The
thoughts fade as Lebechi exhales quite loudly. Six years ago, she
had me enrolled at a rickety hairdressing salon down Zik Street.
Next, she pulled me out and registered me for tailoring lessons
at Madam Dorcas, a shop in the building opposite ours. She
finally withdrew me from the shop before I could even learn to
pedal a sewing machine. In the kitchen one evening, she put
a hand on my shoulder and reassured me that she had bigger
plans for me. She thought I believed her, but she didn't suspect
that I could tell she was a tortoise, craftier than any person I
had met in my entire life. If I annoyed her, she would quickly
remind me to remember where I came from, that I would look
as scrawny as a villager had I remained in Oguta tending my
parents' farm. Anytime she said that to me, I wound up feeling

like a wrinkly, aged thing. The truth is that: she only wanted me to have plenty of time to watch over her children. She needed me to serve as a full-time babysitter.

My cousin and his wife know I don't have the head for numbers and all that math, and besides, money has never enticed me, which is why neither of them has ever insisted that I complete my high school education. In all the years I've lived with them, they never wanted me to visit our village, especially during Easter and Christmas holidays, because they couldn't find anybody to babysit their children. They feared that I'd never return to their house. Sadly, my cousin never once asked me what I wanted to do with my life. He believed it was useless to encourage me to speak my mind. It was as though I should have no say in my future while I lived with him and his family. But this much is true: he has been kind enough to house and feed me, and I'm grateful for that.

Also, my cousin never treated me as some neighbours do with their poor relatives—use them like a rag to wipe scum. All of that is now in the past, like the old photographs of me. If you flip through any of those photographs, you'll feel repulsed by how pimply and skinny I used to look. Your jaw will drop now when you see me standing. I'm well-fed, a girl in full bloom, radiant for all the world to behold. I often catch men turning their heads to leer at my backside. Maybe this is part of what is eating at Lebechi's heart: the way I've transformed into a naturally attractive woman. I remember all of this as clearly as the first day when I lugged my bag into their apartment at the age of eleven.

"I want to smoke," Papa suddenly announces, brandishing a pack of Marlboro.

What made me even think he would ever quit smoking? Not even Mama's "lecturing"—as he calls it—had stopped him. When I lived with them in the village, he had joked that he would rather smoking finished him off than her acidic tongue.

Mama turns to face him. *"Chukwu ekwela,"* she cries, snapping her fingers. "You cannot hold yourself for just one hour?" She comes off as a little too dramatic, as though Papa just declared that he was lighting up the couch.

I'd be glad if they squabbled. That might shift the attention away from me, if only for a moment. I wipe the smile off my face.

Papa gets up in a huff, his breaths surging. "Woman, would the heavens collapse if you allowed me," he pinches the air for emphasis, "just one minute of peace?"

Mama regards him with distaste. Her lips shrink from her teeth. "One minute. One minute. As if forever is even enough for you. You never take anything seriously. We wouldn't be here trying to clean this mess on our hands if you did. If you did what any..."

"...any what?" Papa butts in, his voice climbing sharply. "Don't you start insulting me here, woman."

"...any father would do. But no, no, no. You can't think past yourself. It's all about you. So long as you have something to drink or smoke, the rest of us can jump into the ocean or go straight to hell. That is the only way you know how to think. It is you. You. You. And you." Mama ends her outburst, hissing loudly. She shifts sideways, turning her back to him.

"What is the meaning of all this now?" my uncle asks, frowning. "Is this what we've come here to do? Put each other down in the presence of our children?"

My parents ignore his remarks and continue to squabble. My cousin and his wife look uncomfortable. I suspect that they'd rather sit anywhere else than right here among adults misbehaving in their living room. Their parents know how spiteful my parents can be to each other. But Nonso and Lebechi are only just seeing for the first time this other side of my parents. After all, they rarely visit the village—unlike their own parents.

"Agnes?" Papa calls, but Mama keeps mute. "Agnes? I'm talking to you, Agnes."

Mama completely ignores him.

"Look at me when I'm talking to you," Papa goads her. "You should have been a lecturer with that sharp mouth of yours running like a truck without any brakes."

Mama glances over her shoulder and scoffs at him. "All right, tell me. Maybe I've grown blind, but what's there to look at?" Her eyes rake the length of his lanky body.

My uncle calls both of my parents' names several times; still, they refuse to answer him. His wife tries to intervene, but no one listens to her either.

Mama's silence provokes Papa some more. He edges closer to her and prods her shoulder with his knuckles. At this, she leaps instantly to her feet and thrusts her finger in his face.

"Polycarp, keep your dirty hands to yourself!" The pitch of her voice sends a shudder down my spine.

When Papa attempts to fight back, he sounds like his own voice has cracked. He may as well have been squeaking. "Everything is war with you." He brushes her finger away from his face.

Mama glowers at him before plonking herself back onto the couch. Papa draws away from her and turns to his brother. My uncle's face is one large puff of displeasure.

"Polycarp, how many times have I called you?" he reproaches Papa.

"Sir Knight, you've seen it all for yourself." Papa speaks like he's resigned to not having his way, a man whom everyone constantly disregards in conversations. "It's good you've seen what I have been forced to put up with all these years. There's no peace for me at home. If I want to smoke, she'll complain. If I want to drink, she'll complain. I hope she'll complain when I die."

"Calm down, Polycarp. You're not dying any time soon. And nobody is saying you shouldn't smoke." My uncle motions him to sit down. "This was not what I expected when I called for a family meeting. I cancelled several lucrative appointments to handle this issue. That said, let's get this issue over with, then you can smoke anything you like—"

"It's just one smoke, Sir Knight." Papa interrupts him and, waving the pack of cigarettes, turns to my cousin and his wife as though he craves their support. "See what has happened when I said I needed a smoke?"

I remain quiet, wishing my parents would stop acting stupidly before our relatives.

My uncle blows air out through his lips, appearing as though he's trying not to lose his patience. "Polycarp, I believe we have a more important issue at hand. We're here to resolve that issue. As St. Nicholas is my witness," he jabs a finger in the air, "we haven't even begun to address *it*."

Papa's arms fall limply to his sides. He hangs his head in defeat. Then he finally shoves the pack of cigarettes into his pocket and perches on the other end of the couch. He cradles his head in his hands like he is nursing a headache caused by Mama.

"Your devices cannot work here, Satan," my uncle's wife interjects in the silence that follows. Her face is tilted to the ceiling as though she is addressing the evil manipulator. "You are a liar. You will never tear this family apart."

The living room has grown warmer against my neck. The air feels scorched, even with the windows open wide and the fan blowing hard. I feel my cheeks flushing. Maybe my body is generating too much heat. I slouch in my seat, and shame suddenly takes hold of me. My parents disgraced themselves here because I caused it. Their contempt for me now will only heighten.

I feel like a cornered hen. It is okay that they think I'm ungrateful. Hopeless, I close my eyes. I'll never get the life I wanted, I guess.

My cellphone gives a *cuckoo-o-o* peal just then. I check the caller's ID, and my heart erupts in delight. Yet I'm afraid to answer the call. My uncle clears his throat. I catch Papa twisting his lips in distaste.

Lowering my gaze, I press the "Busy" button. The phone rings again. I clutch it with sweating palms and try not to surrender to panic. I hit the busy button again. My calf muscles stiffen as I pray the phone doesn't ring a third time.

The vibration hits my fingertips—and the whole of my arms becomes a wire—before I hear the beep. A simple text message. As I read the concern in Brother Tobiah's message, the muscles in my calves loosen. He is asking how I am holding up, what decision my family has taken, if any. His message ends with *Ogadinma.* Everything will be all right. That he is concerned, I think, is all that matters for now. I picture him smiling and typing this simple message, and I am reassured by his concern.

Some church sisters wonder why I chose Brother Tobiah over more handsome brothers. He is squat, cheerful, undemanding, and has travelled relatively widely across the country. Life has stretched him long and hard, and his skin is thin and taut like old leather. Crinkles press the sides of his eyes whenever he smiles. He is an orphan, but he has such a generous soul. It is like hardship has softened him and made him tender and sensitive. He would sacrifice his last piece of bread rather than watch you go hungry. You could count on him to jump into the river if a child were drowning.

Unlike my cousin, Brother Tobiah has had to struggle his entire life since no father handed down a portion of his wealth to him. He hawked sausage rolls on the streets of Lagos, sold roasted plantain and fish at motor parks in Port Harcourt, tilled yam farms in Otukpo, and once worked as a butcher in abattoirs in Kano. Yet he never begrudges anyone their privileges or opportunities. He's more content than my cousin could ever be, even with all his education, class, and comforts. Although no man has supported him in the last few decades, Brother Tobiah remains very determined to make a name for himself.

I believe he will. He also believes so because he assures me that things have turned around for the better since I entered his life.

*Ogadinma*—the word is a blessing. From heaven. I breathe in, feeling energized. I stare from one face to another. Yes, I can be my kind of somebody. Nobody's expectations will choke me any longer. Oh yes, my family can put me down all they want. Call me stupid from here to Damascus, but I will not let them make me feel like I'm worthless.

I realize too late that I'm smiling, for my family members swap glances with one another. They no longer look scandalized or horrified. They slung questions at me:

"Where's the idiot? What does he do? Eunice, I hope he isn't one of those charlatans looking for a family to scam?"

"Is he an *osu*? Is his mother a witch?"

"Hope his father is somebody! They have somebody in their lineage, eee?"

"Are his sisters married? Are they divorced?"

The questions quicken my pulse. I take deep breaths. I feel lightheaded, like I've just completed a round of feet-stamping prayers at a vigil.

"He is not a charlatan."

Everyone looks taken aback by the confidence in my voice.

Someone gives a low mocking laugh.

"So, what is he?"

I sit upright. "He's working to be a pastor."

"A w-what?" Mama stutters, leaning forward in her seat.

"A pastor," I repeat, unmoved by her agitation.

Mama grips her shabby headscarf, crumpling it in her hands. "What use is a pastor to our family? I know the devil lives in you." She sounds too dramatic again. "Always known you were sent to torment me. No good for anything."

"Eunice, what kind of pastor impregnates a little girl? How can a pastor do *this* to you?" my uncle's wife asks, slanting her lips.

I see the overblown look of disgust in her eyes. I wouldn't be surprised if she were secretly pleased with my situation. Some women are like that, gleeful over other women's woes.

The lights suddenly go off.

I feel like giggling in the darkness when my uncle curses in Igbo. "*Ndi ara.* That's what you get when you install idiots in government. What rubbish!"

Nonso turns on his cellphone flashlight, cautiously wends his way to the balcony where his generator sits and cranks it on. We hear a clang. The lights flood back into the room. I squeeze my eyes shut then blink to adjust my vision to the yellow glare of the bulbs. Nonso plops himself back onto the couch with a sigh. He steals a glance at his father. Then he turns to stare at me—or through me.

I can practically *see* his thoughts: Brother Tobiah has been fooling around in my house while pretending to study the scripture with you? Sneaking down your skirt while muttering the Lord's Prayer?

Brother Tobiah sometimes pops in while my cousin and his wife are at work. Their children like clinging to him whenever they find him with me. He also enjoys clowning around with them. I often switch on the TV to distract them with cartoons. The instant I notice that the screen has grabbed their attention, Brother Tobiah and I will sit on the couch and study the Bible. Usually, I stretch out on the couch with my head on his lap while he leans back, his hand stroking my shoulder. Always, his words soothe me. There were times when we listened to the audio version of the scripture on his cellphone, though it was never as soothing as his voice. Other times, we spoke about the future, imagining us cuddling in a place of our own. In those intimate moments, I never cared how plain or sparse our living room looked. What our imagination offered us was good enough; we were content with our future, and we believed in each other. What could be more satisfying than that? But Brother Tobiah always left—an hour earlier to give me enough time to put the couch and kitchen back in order—before my cousin or his wife returned from work. *Bread eaten in secret,* he'd whisper in my ear before shutting the door behind him.

The memories tickle me, but I don't giggle. It is no use disrespecting the calm in the room nor adding more kerosene to flames. Gently, I place both palms over my belly. I will miss my cousin's cuddly twins, but I'm more excited to see my own creation in the flesh.

Papa begins to laugh. "He's not a charlatan." He mimics me in a playful nasal tone as if he has stuff in his nostrils. He shakes his head and repeats, "He's not a charlatan," again and again until Mama, bristling, tells him to shut up.

My uncle heaves himself up. His chin folds into his neck as he plods back and forth across the living room. His arms jiggle behind his back, his face a mass of thoughts.

Meanwhile, hunger pangs attack my stomach. The garden eggs and kola nuts are still untouched. The drinks, too.

I glance at the clock; it is past two.

Seriously?

This drama has lasted over two hours!

A wasp finds its way into the living room. It dances over the tray then perches on a kola nut. It lingers there a moment and eventually whizzes off. I follow the wasp with my eyes until it crosses the window. I long to fly away too.

"Is he willing to marry you?" asks my uncle.

I hold his gaze. I know he has long since written me off as some pest to be ignored. Before I can answer him, the twins dart out of their bedroom screaming. One of them runs up to me. Looking up at me, he lifts his arm and feels my brow.

"Aunty, are you ill?" he asks, frowning.

Of course, I am, I want to blurt out, but I rub his hair and tell him I'm fine. He smiles as he inspects the living room. Then he slides across the floor to where his brother is nestling at the feet of their mother. My uncle narrows his eyes at his grandsons.

"You two, go back to your room," Nonso says to his boys, avoiding eye contact with his father.

The twins turn to him and chorus, "No! No! No!"

Nonso hardens his face and snarls, "Come on, go inside."

The twins furrow their lips and stamp their feet on the floor. At last, they scoot back to their room, shrieking, "You're being mean, Dad."

After they've left, my uncle repeats his question to me.

I deliberately hesitate. First, I admire his shiny black shoes, wondering how he can live so comfortably with himself while his brother is dirt poor. Then I gaze up at the open arms of Jesus in the framed photograph on the wall. *Come unto me, O you of the heavy heart* is written in white block letters beneath his burning crimson heart. I've stared at Jesus several times. I only notice now that his blue eyes beam with understanding.

I stroke my belly tenderly. Oddly, not one of my family members has asked if I am happy about my situation. It's only raw indignation they've so far expressed. They think that I must choose to serve another boss when I could just as effortlessly become a boss of my own. Why can't I be trusted enough to decide for myself? Lead life on my terms? I'm willing to trade a life of salary for the position of a full-time pastor's wife without so much as missing a heartbeat.

"He is willing," I finally respond.

"*Ọ gwụla*. It is settled then," my uncle concludes with a sweep of his left hand. "There's nothing more to say." He sinks his bulk into the couch and begins to thumb his cellphone. He appears satisfied with the resolution like he had known before-hand that I'd follow my heart. He might also have known that I was soon going to break free from his son's grasp without help.

"*Uwaemebiela*," Papa wails like he's boasted to his friends about me, only to have me completely humiliate him.

For me, at least, the world hasn't crumbled. For them, maybe. They will eventually come around and accept that my dream was never to go anywhere near a university. It's a terrible life to have to slave away behind any office desk from eight to five. That's why I vowed not to end up like my elder sister, sad-faced and pining for a man. Or like Nonso either, who complains about too much work and little pay. Not like his wife, who wishes she didn't have to work but must anyway because she earns a fraction more than her husband. Busyness and discontent often go together, I learned from watching them.

What were my options in life? I had no answers at the time. Yet, as every believer knows, as we steadfastly believe, our Lord works in sundry and mysterious ways, and I'm a witness to His mystery.

Good fortune came my way one Sunday after the morning service at church. I had gone to pick up my cousin's twins from the children's section when Brother Tobiah gestured to me. I stalled and wondered who he was. Then, with the boys in tow, I walked over to where he sat on a stool opposite the admin office. He stood up and offered me his seat. I liked the gaudy emerald kaftan he wore. He made funny faces at the boys, and they giggled uncontrollably. His fondness for them gave me some goosebumps, the good kind. We spoke briefly but warmly. Brother Tobiah didn't seem judgemental. He sounded like a brother who would still dote on a wayward sister.

I still remember what he told me then: "You're beloved of God, Sister Eunice." The following Sunday at church, we chatted again, much longer this time. "Sister Eunice, you have a gracious heart, free of guile." Before my cousin and his family drove out of the church premises that day, Brother Tobiah promised to help push me along the right path. Since then, he has been nurturing my faith.

My mind jolts back to the present when Mama rises noisily from the couch. She doesn't even look at me. She thanks my uncle and his wife, apologizes for the embarrassment her family has caused, and then announces, "I'm going."

"Thank you, Sir Knight," Papa says, lurching off the couch. A cloud hovers on his face, and he looks shattered.

Nonso and his wife get up from their seats, beaming with relief. My uncle's wife remains seated, quietly watching the movements around her.

I suddenly want Papa to insult me—spit out his bile, so long as it will make him feel better, but nothing will. I close my eyes and try to ignore my thumping heart. That's when I feel the first nudge in my womb—my baby is just five months old and already has such powerful kicks.

Who can say?

He may become a soccer player. Maybe he'll play for the Nigerian Dream Team. Or better still, he could leave the country and play for one of the European soccer clubs.

What more could I wish for?

A simple enough dream if you like.

# FACE LIKE A MASK

Before I could race out of my room, the front door flew open—and shadows attacked our living room. They have come, I thought and jumped off the bed. I wished I had the handgun in my hands right now, which was hidden in the couch's stuffing. I crept to the living room where it was, and I stood still. The air stank of carbide. I knew that smell. It always hung in the air after CRODEF and the army had exchanged fire.

Pa and Ma scrambled out of their room. As soon as they saw the shadows, they sprang back at once as if they'd stepped on nails. Sleep had left our house. Nobody, not even Pa, whose snores normally crackled like burning firewood, would shut his eyes ever again. My brother had prepared me for a day like this, but I hadn't expected that it would happen so soon, in the dead of night. He'd forewarned our parents, too, but Pa was as stubborn as a stump.

The shadows took the form of six hefty men; they circled our centre table. Bob Marley continued to play on the radio in my parents' bedroom. Pa often left the radio on until the FM station closed and only increased the volume higher than usual to block out the noises he and Ma made in bed.

Pa stood trembling in front of Ma, who hugged his arm. I wished Bro Willy was around to blast the men out of the door with his short gun.

"Use it. Protect yourself," he'd told me, folding my fingers around the handgun. A nine-millimetre. It had chilled my palm, but I was excited because I longed to defend our village, too. "Remember, Timi. Use it right." He gave me a few practice lessons in the bush. That was a week ago before he disappeared from the village.

Now Bro Willy's words pushed me to the couch where I had hidden the gun. Before I could reach it, a hand gripped my ankle, and I found myself hanging upside down like a bat. My fingers scraped the floor. Blood pumped behind my eyeballs.

I couldn't place the strange face in the tiny flicker of the lantern.

"Please, please," Pa begged. "Let him go."

The stranger cackled like a hyena.

My free leg kicked in the air. The hand around my ankle tossed me across the room. I felt the pain before my bottom hit the floor. It was raw, the pain—it pierced through to my anus. I crept away, wishing I had kept the gun under my bed.

One of the men marched over to the table. I thought he was going to turn off the lantern, but he turned it up instead.

The room glowed a soft orange like the River Nun at sunset.

The men were dressed in mufti, with bullets forming belts across their waists. Their huge frames gave them a look of death, and I shivered in the hotness of our stuffy room. They looked like members of CRODEF, though they didn't wear masks. Besides, there had never been stories of CRODEF breaking into people's homes at midnight. The men looked nothing like soldiers, though it was hard to tell in the dark. Something like soot was smeared on their faces. They watched us silently like they were drinking in Bob Marley's music. I remembered Bro Willy had called their tactics *mind games.*

"*Abei*, where's that *shcrap*?" One of them finally spoke, the man who'd slammed me to the ground. The leader, I suspected, by the way he barked at the others.

"I don't know who you're looking for." Pa had never once stuttered a day in his life. Now his teeth chattered and his words bumped into each other.

Ma let go of Pa's arm and began yelling the name of God. Her shouts drowned out Bob Marley's voice. If we survived the night, I knew she would never forgive Pa. She'd begged him several times to move. Half of our people had relocated to neighbouring villages. No one wanted to live around such violence. "Close your shatty mouth."

The leader marched toward Ma, wrenched her away from Pa's side, and flung her to the floor. His machine gun edged close to her temple. He threatened to shatter her skull if she kept yelling. Ma lay unmoving on the floor as if she had already passed out.

I imagined her brains scattered across the torn carpet, a sticky mess, like the time I had pulped a mudfish with my shoe. And I suddenly felt dizzy.

"You'd rather I lock your loud mouth with bullets?"

Ma had lost her voice.

"Please, please, don't hurt her." Pa raised a hand.

"Shat up!" The leader barked at him.

Pa pressed his legs together, his hands wrapped around the back of his neck.

The leader swung his head around. "Look for that piece of shat."

The men bounded like dogs into Pa's room. They turned everything upside down. I heard the clatter of metal, plastic, wood, the smash of glass. I knew they were looking for my elder brother.

Pa had warned him a few days earlier: "Leave those people. I have only two of you."

Bro Willy had replied, "Pa, chill. Nothing will happen."

When Ma pleaded with Bro Willy to quit all his fighting, he put an arm over her shoulders. "Is this the kind of land you want to leave for your grandchildren, Ma?" he asked. "No water, no light, no road? No farm. No river. No market. Poison in the air we breathe. Oil on the water we drink. Look at Odi. Look around."

His speech had left Ma in a bad mood. Later that evening, she had ended up cursing AGIP, Shell, and the other oil companies at the dinner table.

The leader stamped over to Pa. His height made Pa look like a dwarf. My heart hammered, but anger had begun to rise in place of dread as I crouched in the corner. He gripped Pa by the shoulder and pulled him to his feet.

"Where's your bastard son?"

I wanted to tell him that Bro Willy had gone away, but I wasn't sure who they were. Ever since CRODEF became popular, many other groups had also sprung up and taken over the struggle. We now had real and fake freedom fighters. Everybody was fighting to free our land from the "curse of black gold."

"I-I have not seen him in three days," Pa sputtered as if he was choking.

"Three days? Do I look like a fool to you?" asked the leader.

"No, sir, I swear."

This wasn't a rogue militant group. These were government forces, the people who beat up villagers. Our "oppressors," as the old village men had nicknamed them. But why did they disguise themselves as CRODEF?

"Lie next to her," the leader ordered.

Pa dropped to the floor and stretched himself out. Anger crept into my throat. I balled my fists and silently cursed the governor's mother. Bro Willy had told me that the traitor had allowed the president to talk him into attacking his own people. After the army fell upon our village, everything had gone crazy. Goats and fowl had disappeared. Men were beaten or shot down. Girls, dragged by soldiers into tarpaulin tents, came out bleeding and sobbing.

Now the dogs leaped out from my parents' bedroom, barking. I smelled the stink of their sweat and hemp. I wondered where any CRODEF members were. How could they not hear all this noise? This would make a perfect ambush. I imagined CRODEF slaughtering them all.

"We can't find him," one of the men said.

"He's fled," said another.

"Fled?" The leader sounded stunned. He punched a fist into his palm to make a soft sucking sound. "Where is Willy?" His voice threatened to bring down the rafters of our house.

Bro Willy hid his guns, wrapped in an old *abo*, on one side of the ceiling. You couldn't see the loose boards unless it was daylight. I had secretly watched him while he hid the guns there. I bet he was hiding in CRODEF's hideout, the same hideout he'd described to me many times. If anything happened, I was to look for him there.

The leader crooked his finger at his men. They gathered around him and whispered. I wished I could snatch the gun lying under the couch, click it the way Bro Willy had shown me, and blast these brutes to hell and beyond.

A man slid away from the group and asked Pa, "Where's your bastard son?"

"I don't know."

The man growled.

For a second, I thought he was going to drag Pa out of the room and put a bullet in his forehead. Like the hole in Sekibo's head when a fisherman hauled him out of the river. That was last year. The soldiers had arrived from Port Harcourt, and Sekibo had been drinking with some boys at a pub when they attacked them. Only a few of them had escaped; the rest had their bodies perforated with bullets.

"Maybe if I pump some bullets into your shit hole, you'll speak?"

"Don't kill me, please," Pa squeaked as the man pressed a boot into his backside.

"Where is Willy-the-bastard-Willy?" the leader demanded. His frustration smelled rubbery, like the slick on the river.

I wondered what Bro Willy had done to him. Had he done anything at all besides fight against the oil company? Once, I overheard him and his friend whispering about a contact in the governor's office. Maybe I had misheard him.

"I don't know." Pa's voice wobbled.

"Shat, shat. SHAT UP!" The leader banged his fist on the table, sending the lantern to the floor.

I thought the globe would shatter, but it didn't. Even the flame didn't go out. A hand reached for it and set it back on the table. I caught a glimpse of the emblem, a metal cross, gleaming on the leader's chest.

My jaw dropped.

I had seen that cross a couple of times before, when I'd searched Bro Willy's pockets for loose change. The cross belonged to his group, but he had always kept it hidden. I squinted at the men's faces and finally recognized that they weren't our oppressors but members of my brother's group, the Cross of the Delta Emancipation Force.

With my chest tight, I remembered Bro Willy describing how they had blown up a few Shell and AGIP gas plants. They had laid out dynamites and then set them off by phone. It had sounded like fun to me at the time. I was always thrilled listening to him and picturing my brother like Rambo gunning down the bloody soldiers.

My bladder burned when I recognized the giant standing over my parents—the famous Gagala. A man whose name made people glance around frantically or run away if they had any reason to believe they were on his bad side. He used to be a bouncer at a nightclub in Warri. Then the former governor hired him as a hitman and bodyguard. I hadn't even laid eyes on him until now, but every boy my age wanted to be as brave as Gagala.

The guns!

Understanding hit me. That's what was driving Gagala mad, I thought. He was here to retrieve the guns that Bro Willy had displayed before me last month. Bro Willy boasted that the group had always tasked him with picking up weapons from its supplier in Port Harcourt. I remembered him carrying an AK-47. The perfect girl, Bro Willy had called it.

"Shat that radio off!"

Someone walked into my parents' room.

Pa gasped as the radio whizzed through the doorway and shattered into pieces. Bob Marley's voice vanished. Pa loved that radio. He liked listening to the news. He laughed when the government made threats through its spokesperson. He said the jackass president couldn't stop our boys. It was from the radio that Pa heard the president calling our boys terrorists. Pa said he was an *abugo*—a stinky, big-nosed monkey. The president was lucky because our boys didn't blow themselves up on buses or in the markets and schools like some youths did in faraway countries. How could the jackass call their people terrorists?

"The thief isn't here," a boy said.

The boy couldn't have been more than seventeen, but he was tall and well-built. He had a red bandana tied around his head. Pointing his gun at the floor, he turned and kicked Pa in the ribs.

Pa gave a cry that reminded me of our dog's howl when a car ran him over two months ago.

Clawing at his shoulders, Gagala let out a deep sound like water burbling down the drain. I imagined him driving a fist into the wall, creating a big hole twice the size of my fist. He stamped over to where I lay curled up on the floor. He grunted hard so that his body shook like a wounded beast.

I suddenly needed to pee, but I stayed still. I didn't want him to get angrier.

Pa remained trembling on the floor. Would we suffer whatever punishment Gagala had intended for Bro Willy?

"Please, leave him, please," Pa pleaded, his voice grainy. He was probably regretting not moving us the first time Ma had suggested it. He was proud of Bro Willy, even though he understood that the government wanted to get rid of CRODEF.

Gagala glared at him. Then, bending down, his eyes levelled with mine. "How old are you?"

"He's only a small boy." Ma sounded unafraid, like she finally had accepted that the worse could happen, and it was useless fighting it.

"Fifteen," I said.

Gagala blew air into my face. The scars on his own face lent him a deadly look—jagged grooves on his cheek, jaw, and under his eye. It was hard not to tremble before him.

I was getting afraid that I'd pee in front of them all.

"Someone must know something about Willy the Bastard," he muttered.

I knew what Bro Willy would have said if he were around, so I said it. "Don't kill my father. Don't kill my mother. We are one with CRODEF."

Gagala and his men stared at me.

I kept my face like a mask, hardened, frozen in one expression— defiance—like Bro Willy's face. I could stay a little calm because he had always told me I had protection. I knew he was referring to Egbesu, our god of war.

Gagala held my chin, tipping it up with his index finger.

I didn't flinch, though his eyes burned right through mine. I had seen that look before in a soldier's eye. The soldier and his men had mounted a roadblock on our main road when the government declared *Operation Fish Out and Destroy*—or "The Invasion," as the villagers had called it. The soldier had stopped Ma as we tried to ride by on our bicycles. I'd narrowed my eyes at him. He had grinned and dragged a hand across his neck as if he was slicing someone's throat.

I saw that same look on Gagala's face now. He was going to cut my brother's throat if he ever got hold of him.

"We don't harm families," he said.

I knew he wouldn't hurt me because I wasn't an outsider like the army. Like the white men and their oil companies who first destroyed our farms and rivers.

"We want your brother. He stole from us. Something."

"Bro Willy?" I asked, sure he was referring to the guns.

Gagala nodded.

"Bro Willy stole from you?"

"Guns," he replied. "My guns."

The guns were no longer in the ceiling. I sat up, ashamed of my brother. I thought he'd stolen them from the soldiers. Had he sold out?

"Is there something you want to tell us?"

"Bro Willy is fighting for our land."

Gagala studied my face as if he could read my mind. I thought he seemed quite impressed with my boldness.

"When was the last time you saw him?" he asked.

"I haven't seen him for a long time."

"Were you not with him today?"

I shook my head.

Gagala was quiet.

"I need to pee."

"Smart chimp." He snorted. "Loco, take him along until we get news of Willy's whereabouts."

"No, no, please, take me instead!" Pa cried, rising from the floor.

I saw the sharp sweep of someone's gun. I was afraid that they would blast him between the eyes. The gun struck him on the back of his head, and Pa collapsed on the floor.

Ma screamed and scrambled to her feet.

"Papaaaa," I cried, also rushing over to him.

Someone grabbed my arm, spun me round, and shoved me out the door. I stumbled but quickly righted myself.

The darkness had the thick texture of wool. There was no moon, no stars. A chill grazed my arms. People had long put out their lights so as to not draw attention to their homes. I could hear my parents crying behind me. I longed to run back and pee, to hide under my bed and never come out. I wanted to tell them that I would escape, like Bro Willy did.

Gagala clasped my shoulder. "They can cry from now till tomorrow," he said. "Nobody will hear them." He sounded so sure of himself. His group must have outnumbered and killed the soldiers.

I felt helpless. Bro Willy wasn't coming back for us. He had gone into hiding like a coward.

"You still want to pee?" Gagala asked.

"Yes," I answered. My bladder was still burning.

"There." He pointed at a tree ahead of me.

I stood at the tree and let my pee splash its trunk. For a second, I felt as light as a balloon.

"Keep walking," someone said, snapping his fingers.

I continued walking between the men.

Gagala and his men led me down to the river, where two canoes sat on the shore.

The shadows of trees wavered, as if something was watching our movements. No cricket chirped; no frog croaked. All was silent. Bro Willy had told me that some CRODEF members could change into eels and *egere*—crocodiles—so that they could slip into the water undetected.

I closed my eyes as the men pushed the canoes into the river. I prayed that Bro Willy could sense where we were and change into a water animal. I began picturing him lurking underwater, waiting to turn our canoes over, when a hand jabbed me into one of the canoes. I fell and picked myself up.

I sat with Gagala and two others in a canoe. The water around us rippled as we rowed. It was murky and smelled of rotten fish. The air had grown chillier, darker than bitumen. I don't know how far we sailed because I ended up nodding to sleep.

When I opened my eyes, something shone ahead of us. We'd arrived on shore. I saw lights flickering in a couple of huts huddled close to one another. Palm trees arched over them. The whole place teemed with trees. I could see something loom tall into the sky, like a transmission tower or a crane. In the darkness, I couldn't tell exactly what it was. Maybe I had imagined it.

We walked to the huts, and Gagala stopped in front of one.

"This is your new home," he said, clapping a hand on my shoulder. "Until your brother shows his face. If he isn't in Port Harcourt already, that is."

As Gagala marched off, leaving me with a guard, I looked at Gagala with some pity. I imagined what horrible things the soldiers would do to him and his boys when the soldiers eventually captured them. I gazed around the room made of bamboo and roofed with raffia fronds.

An orange flame peeped out from a used Nescafe tin. Someone had laid a washed-out plank across the bedsprings. No mattress. No blankets.

"In the end, we'll lose." I realized I was repeating Bro Willy's speech. He had spoken those words to me the week he disappeared.

"We kill them. They send more soldiers. We have the oil, but they control our destiny. I will come back for you guys when the soldiers have all gone. If they don't, I'll still return to take all of you with me to Port Harcourt. I promise."

As I thought about Bro Willy, I didn't think I could trust him any longer because he had stolen from his friends with whom he had taken a blood oath. I got angry, then sad. I lay on the plank and gazed off into the half-light.

Then it came to me.

I remembered the secret hideout and its physical markers that Bro Willy had told me about. If the object that loomed above the trees was what I thought it was, I was close.

Very close.

I sat up and pressed my knees together to contain my excitement.

\*

The morning sun hung over the blue sea that frothed at the shore. The wind blew strong among the palm trees as the bandana boy, who had kicked Pa in the ribs, led me to a latrine behind the huts where we'd all spent the night. The boy stood at the zinc door, gun in hand, while I tried to pee.

The hot air stank of rotten flesh, urine, and feces. Flies buzzed around me so ferociously, as if I was a mass of rot myself.

I almost threw up.

I wanted to shove the door open and run straight into the tangle of trees, but the boy would gun me down before I had even covered a yard.

When I reeled out of the latrine, I asked him, "How long will I be here for?"

He gripped the gun hard and said, "Walk."

On our way back to the huts, the sun seemed to shift and point its glare right into my eyes. I glanced away, shielding my face. I stopped walking.

"What's wrong with you?" the boy asked.

I pointed at the sun without raising my head.

He started laughing.

I turned to look at him and caught sight of the object towering beyond the palm trees, the one I hadn't been able to make out the night before. I saw it very clearly now.

A derrick, an old one. It was the hideout marker.

It meant help was on its way; that was what Bro Willy said.

The boy twisted his face in a scowl. "Keep walking," he barked.

I quickened my steps, pretending like the sight of the derrick didn't excite me.

# MOVE ON

You wake up feeling like a slug. Your legs are heavy as you walk to the washroom and unzip your shorts. Your urine is the colour of tea, brown like leaves shrunken by the harmattan. Outside, the dry wind sighs. Zinc roof sheets clatter. You sag into the armchair, sending dust from the cushions into the air. Motes flit before your eyes. And you feel that's what is left of your life now—specks of dust.

You slump in the chair, thinking, Kaiso can't turn me into a mess.

But she already has.

Yesterday was Christmas day. Joyful voices of your drunken friends still pulsate in your head. Kaiso's voice chafes your mind as the event replays itself.

I feel like I'm losing something, Kaiso had said.

What are you talking about? you'd asked.

I'm sorry to say this, Mudi. You must move on without me. It's been five years. I've tried. I can't keep doing this. There's nothing here for me. Nothing to hold on to.

For two nights, you've tried to understand why she left you, why she ditched you. She wouldn't have disappeared had you promised to marry her. You never thought about marriage because you figured it would ruin your relationship. You believed she'd always be around for years, always, even forever.

A bell jangles outside your window. The preacher, who wears a full beard, smelly dreadlocks, and an ancient red coat, crosses the street. His metal cross dangles from his neck. He clutches his weathered Bible, wailing, always wailing like John the Baptist. Once, you considered splashing a bucket of water on him for all the noise he makes every morning.

Now, you try to imagine him as a miracle worker.

Hoisting yourself up, you realize you could do with a miracle this very minute. You don't really believe in miracles, but you grab your cellphone and dial Kaiso's number, praying she answers. It rings and rings, your heart backflipping with anticipation.

You pace around the room, then pause in front of the couch, and redial her number. As it rings once again, you continue walking up and down the room. Press the phone to your ear. If she picks up, you will propose to her.

For the first time since the breakup, you feel deflated, empty even. It's like someone has scooped out your insides to leave behind only a hollow frame. You never knew you could miss another person this much. Remember the first time you met her?

That Friday evening in a Chinese takeout, where you'd gone to pick up some sweet-and-sour chicken for your supervisor? Kaiso had also come to get some takeout food—lemongrass beef and fried rice—and she had caught your attention immediately with her soft, throaty laugh at the counter. You watched her from where you sat at the table, waiting for your own food. As she fished around in her handbag for her card to pay for her order, you quietly glided over to her.

The onion cakes are yummy, you said. You should try them.

No, thanks, she replied without glancing up from her bag.

You smiled, even though she kept a straight face. As she swiped her card on the POS terminal, you carefully chipped in something about delicious shawarma and began to chat about the best takeout in the neighbourhood. It was then that she looked up and flashed a smile at you. While talking, you realized she was from Assa—the same oil-rich village as you. When you finally asked for her phone number, she gave another throaty laugh and reeled off the eleven digits.

You had slept with many women over the years before meeting her that evening, yet none of them could ever replace the special way she moaned your name—Mudd-di—steaming your face with her breath. You realize now that your room won't ring with her tinkling laughs ever again.

You flop back into the chair when Kaiso doesn't answer your calls. Your head lolls to your chest. When she was around, you worried less about things—what to eat, what to wear. Even when your family tried to squeeze every coin from your pores, you had cared very little because she demanded nothing of you except faithfulness. She was like the steam in a mug of cocoa on a chilly night. The eucalyptus balm spread over the stiffness in your neck. The handrail you clung to anytime the bus rocked and pitched over the bumps of life.

Kaiso made you look capable, dressed you up, reminded you to shave, and pared your crooked nails. Every time she walked by your side, you felt your head and chest swell as if she had packed precious stones into your pockets. She spent a large chunk of her paycheque from her customer service job at a mobile phone company on you.

Hey babe, you usually protested. We should save some money.

That's my big baby talking now, she usually replied, brushing you off with a smile.

There was that Black Friday evening when she came back from work and handed you a pair of moccasin suede loafers. You stared at the exquisite shoes, and your whole body melted. No one had ever given you such an expensive gift before. Come to think of it, you don't remember buying her gifts. But now, you wish you had.

You aren't tight-fisted by nature, but the problem stems from Papa, whose diabetes eats up most of your earnings. Plus, your younger siblings' school fees. You can't even recall the number of times you've been tempted to steal food from the university guest house, where you work as a cook. You once wondered if Papa wasn't somehow better off dead.

A sourness creeps onto your tongue, the aftertaste of a breakup. You haven't yet brushed your teeth. Kaiso always reminded you to brush your teeth twice every day. She is the only thing that makes sense in your life.

You sit up.

I should join one of those fast-growing churches, you think. People get rich these days. Quick connections. Maybe that will bring Kaiso back into your arms. She will see that you've changed and grown more responsible.

The bell jangles from outside again.

You consider flinging the phone at the preacher through the window. Instead, you plunk it on the table. And then you think: I'm forty-five years old, not some weepy boy. I won't jump off Third Mainland Bridge for any girl.

Pleased with your decision, you switch on the radio.

It's your time to shine, a voice booms from the speakers.

You cover your ears.

This is your year of prosperity. Financial EXPLOSION!

You reach for the volume knob of the radio but pause.

Can you say ex-plo-sion, dear listeners?

It sounds strange, but it seems that the speaker meant to address you. So you say the word like it's magical, slowly, self-consciously, Explosion.

And strangely, you feel lighter.

Now say amen.

You punch the air with a fist. AMEN!

Moments later, a soft, bone-melting song drifts through the room. You can't help but think the lyrics hold a secret message. The song trails goosebumps along your arms.

*I'm going to let you in...*

The song keeps speaking to you:
*My heart is wide as the sky...*
Your lips move:
*Hold my hand, fly away with me...*
You spin on your heels. Magic, you think. No, a miracle.

You decide right away to quit your job after the New Year holidays. Bye-bye, my dear university. I will not be your silly cook any longer. You aren't sure what next job you'll take on, but you feel confident that your days of meagre living are over.

Something screams outside, and you run straight to the window. The harmattan dust fills your nostrils. You feel warm inside, despite the chilly touch in the air. There is a crowd running up and down the street.

You were stranded at Ojota once. The commercial drivers had gone on a strike because the government had hiked the price of gasoline for the second time in a year. You had watched as humans trudge homewards, ready to attack one another at the slightest shove. Something similar is taking place right now.

Your street overflows with people racing around with buckets and gallons. Two days before, the neighbourhood had noticed a leaking pipeline off Shobowale Street, gasoline pooling underneath. Vandals had dug a hole five-feet deep into the earth. They had drilled into the pipeline and then sped off with a generous quantity of gasoline stacked on their pick-up truck. They sealed the pipeline rather carelessly.

Now men and boys haul large gallons. Women and girls carry small containers, all sagging under the weight of black gold, carting home fortune.

Your heart thumps, thumps, thumps.

Your "Year of Financial Explosion" could start now. Nine years in the city has finally yielded fruits!

You find yourself...
*cruising around your village in a BMW*
*your mother crying hallelujah*

*girls flocking around you*
*children running after...*
In a flash, you empty the water in your 50-litre gallon.

Outside, you almost bump into the dreadlocked preacher.

Sorry, you pant.

Son, remember, he says with a cackle. There shall be weeping and gnashing of teeth, for man is born unto trouble.

You ignore him, thinking of the day you will cut off his beard.

Young and old men and women nudge one another around the pipeline. Mothers with babies strapped to their backs strain harder to scoop the precious amber liquid into metal containers.

The fumes sting your eyes worse than ground red pepper would. In your mind, you are busy counting banknotes while Kaiso hovers excitedly behind you. Her throaty laughter evokes an image of her stroking your cheek while you nibble at her belly button.

Your back and knees crackle as you straighten up. Success comes with a cost. The gasoline-soaked ground shimmers with rainbows. The story of Noah comes to mind and leaves you smiling. A plastic bag lies at your feet. You snatch it and wrap it over the mouth of the gallon.

Tighten the cap.

You lug your treasure.

Squeeze your body between the hoods of cars, nosing one another. Weave your way through the swelling mass like a crab. So much elbowing, jostling for space.

A police officer gives you an envious look, but you're in too much of a jubilant mood to care.

A woman cries out in pain.

A man asks her why she is moving so slowly.

Someone taps you.

You turn around and see the sweat-drenched man pointing left.

These okada boys, the man gushes. They drive like demons!

A motorcyclist zooms toward the crowd, which parts immediately like the Red Sea. Two boys gripping four gallons sit behind the motorcyclist.

Get off the way, scavengers! one of them barks.

Maniacs, you curse, dropping your gallon and scurrying sideways.

Tiny sparks fly off the rear tire of the motorbike.

An eerie sensation chills your forearms. Bracing yourself, you heave the gallon onto your head. You wobble. Before you can steady yourself, an explosion surges so powerfully that it lifts you off your feet.

Later, after the fire had raged for an entire day and finally died out, neighbours will gather on their veranda and ask who had started it. Some will blame the devil for the fire. Others will say it was the hands of God. And a few will say it was all a mighty mystery.

But for now, voices rise and fall over each other—panic screams through the air.

Your head slams against the hood of a car. You swirl in darkness for a while. Eyes pop open as you smell blood on your lips.

The motorcycle smoulders in an orange blaze. The teenagers writhe and yell. Men, women, and children flail about like beheaded chickens. Everyone is bumping into one another. A danfo bus draped in hundreds of posters of the president barrels into a dumpster.

The electric lines suddenly sputter.

Smoke billows into the morning sky.

You try to rise, but the effort hurts. You're tired.

At last, you stagger to your feet. But something like wool crams your chest. Its grip reaches up to tighten around your neck. You swat at it, only for your fingers to grasp fumes. The hairs in your nostrils feel singed.

Your eyes begin to water, and you struggle to blink and keep them open.

Then your knees buckle.

And you collapse in coughs, gasping for breath.

As the hungry flames leap at you with a roar, Kaiso's voice rings out,

Don't move on, darling.

# JOURNEY

H e is going to be all right," the bearded man said.
"Who will be?" asked Jaya.

Bearded Man didn't respond. Instead, he levelled his eyes on the bus driver and ignored Jaya.

Great, his seatmate just talked to himself? There were about five or six passengers on the bus, looking composed, somewhat cheerful. Maybe his seatmate was going crazy. He could jump off the bus, for all Jaya cared. The country had gone crazy, after all. What difference would it make?

There was always news about bandits attacking neighbourhoods, banks, and highways. A gang had even ransacked a church! It was common these days to hear on the radio that a woman had stabbed her sleeping husband. A partner had bathed their lover with acid. Upon losing his job, a father had jumped off a bridge and into a river. There was the mother who leaped in front of a speeding truck. Police officers had arrested a clique of students with bags of fresh human organs in one nightclub. A python had swallowed millions of banknotes in a government office.

Jaya huffed quietly to himself. He still remembered the story of the notorious armed robber nicknamed Django, whom vigilantes had trapped in a dead-end street only for him to have quickly transformed himself into a goat.

These were crazy times indeed.

Bearded Man cleared his throat. At that moment, he turned and glanced sharply at Jaya. In the few seconds that it lasted,

Jaya found his gaze disconcerting. It was as if his seatmate had heard Jaya's thoughts.

"I can't say the same about you." Bearded Man avoided eye contact as he spoke. "But your boy will be fine."

A shudder passed through Jaya's body, and his hands jerked at his sides. How did his seatmate know about his bedridden son? Except for him and his wife, no one, not even their neighbours, knew about the boy's condition. He and his wife had fed their son paracetamol and anti-malaria tablets, but still, the fever had shown no sign of leaving his thin body. He had convinced his wife that they should manage the illness at home until he returned from his trip.

Jaya wasn't supposed to go on this trip. He had found it difficult to sleep at night ever since his plumbing business went under two months ago. His wife barely made enough money selling tomatoes. Every now and then, he battled nightmares of his family living under the bridge and starving to death. He felt helpless, even desperate, as if he had lost his voice, but he managed not to panic, which was also a battle on its own. Because his son's illness consumed most of his miserable earnings, he vowed to get any job so long as it involved neither murder nor theft.

So, when he called his cousin in Abuja for possible contacts, he learned of a job and the hefty pay that came with it. No desperate man could say no to that kind of money, especially if they had a wife and a sick child. Jaya believed that the pay could save his family.

It was a simple job, discreet and fun.

"Do I know you? Have we met before?"

Jaya prodded Bearded Man, who neither looked at him nor said anything else. The man had a long, unblemished face. Jaya found his silence a little rude, but he let the man be. He was sure that their paths had crossed before and that his seatmate knew him from somewhere. Or maybe he had overheard the phone conversation between Jaya and his wife some moments ago. Otherwise, how else would he know about his son?

Jaya's new client had insisted that they meet up this weekend before her trip abroad. She had promised to get him some chocolates for his son when she returned to Nigeria in a fortnight, but only if he remained her "good teddy bear." They were going to meet for the first time, and he hoped to make a load of money off her.

From the last row of seats, someone gave a sudden cry.

"Stop! I want to get off," a girl in a pink blouse insisted.

"Stop where?" said a boy with a Mohawk haircut.

"Your head correct so?" another boy said, tapping at his head. Jaya saw a tattoo of a cobra on his forearm and his calves stiffened. "He should stop you in the goddamn bush, so you can do what?"

A stray thought crept into Jaya's mind. Fear clamped his stomach, clawing into his intestines. His breath shortened, and he tried not to look alarmed in the presence of his fellow passengers.

He had considered not going on this trip, he reminded himself. While heading to the bus station at seven, he had suspected it would rain. The clouds loomed heavy and grey, and he imagined it could be a sign for him to cancel the trip. His wife would have insisted that it was an omen had she been the one to see it. He tried not to believe in such *unreasonable* things, despite her insistence. It was August, after all, and it hadn't rained for two or more weeks. In the end, Jaya told himself that he was only nervous because he would be cheating on his wife for the first time. He felt terrible leaving her alone to look after their ailing son. He'd make it up to her once he returned from his trip.

But now, Jaya remembered stories told in pubs about passengers who tricked drivers on transit, only for armed men to launch out of the blue, pouncing on everyone onboard the moment the bus slowed to a halt. He darted his eyes around, scanning faces to see if any passenger seemed out of place. He sighed with relief when the driver questioned the girl in pink.

"Young lady, what are you saying?" In the rear-view mirror, the driver watched the girl inching her way forward along the aisle.

"Driver, focus," said a man with glasses who sat in front with the driver. He didn't peel his eyes from his newspaper.

The girl bent down in the aisle by the door. Her hand hovered over its lever. "I will push open the door."

"Open the goddamn door, and I'll push you outside myself," Tattoo Boy said.

His threat drew a curtain of brooding silence over everyone. Jaya wasn't sure that they weren't going to be robbed, but he wondered why Bearded Man just sat there untouched by the drama—as though the bus could flip four times on its head, and he still wouldn't bat an eyelash.

A woman in sequinned jeans said to the girl, "You want to jump?" She and the couple in matching print attire sat in the first row of seats behind the driver.

The girl eyed her back. "My sister said I should come down—"

Fellow passengers immediately volleyed questions at her, cutting her short. She looked like a cornered rabbit.

Jaya came to her aid and asked her if she knew where she was headed. She hesitated, then gave a shake of her head. He doubted that an eighteen- year-old could get on a bus and not know where she was going.

She must have seen the look on his face because she asked, "Is this bus not going to Lagos?"

"Lagos?" Mohawk Boy spat, twisting his nose as though the word stank.

Tattoo Boy echoed him, dropping his jaw in disbelief.

Jaya wondered whether she was on the wrong bus because she wasn't in her right mind.

The other passengers looked baffled, too, except for Bearded Man. They regarded each other in stunned silence like they were the butt of a joke. Then Mohawk Boy and Tattoo Boy laughed hard, veins sticking out in their necks. They called the girl names like bucket head and chewing stick. They tried to goad her into tears. She remained silent, clutching the door lever.

Jaya knew better than to hush them for being mean in case they turned on him as well.

"Driver. Focus, focus," said Glasses.

The couple told the girl to sit her butt down.

She still insisted on getting off the bus. "My sister is on another bus."

Jaya asked her, "Where are you and your sister going?"

"Lagos."

"This bus is going to Abuja. Call your sister."

The girl frowned and then fiddled with her cellphone before dialling a number. She reeled off a flurry of Owerri dialect, a melodious nasal drawl. Something her sister said on the phone made her face crumple.

The driver asked to speak with her sister. He reached one hand out behind him while the other continued to tightly grip the steering wheel.

The girl held her phone out across the rows of seats.

Before it could get to the driver, Mohawk Boy snatched it from her.

Placing the phone on his ear, he growled, "What are you girls up to…?"

"Guy. Guy, relax." The driver tried to calm him down. "Let me speak with her."

"Driver. Can you just focus, please?" Glasses sounded annoyed.

The driver ignored him. He took the phone from Mohawk Boy and spoke with the girl's sister. Without taking his eyes off the road, he thrust the phone behind him to someone.

Sequinned Jeans reached for it and handed it over to the girl.

"I'll drop you off at Agbor junction," the driver said. "Wait there for your sister. Her bus is ten or twenty minutes behind us." He started humming to himself.

"Can't even say a goddamn thank you," Tattoo Boy hissed when the girl shuffled back to her seat.

Only Jaya and his seatmate kept silent while the others joked about the situation. Mohawk Boy asked his friend what he had expected from a girl with a face like yam-bread. Laughing, Sequinned Jeans asked if there was ever a thing like yam-bread, to which he replied yes.

The couple in matching attire also laughed. Husband spoke of girls who snuck away with their friends to go sleep with Indians in Lagos. Wife added that every Indian man who slept with those girls had stolen their wombs to make charms.

Glasses snapped his fingers. He recalled aloud what he had read in the dailies about the police freeing some schoolgirls from a hotel where they were to be shipped like sardines to Italy and Saudi Arabia.

"God's wrath is coming in a storm," he said, with the air of finality typical of a roadside prophet.

A soulful song about heartbreak began to play on the radio. It filled Jaya with a fuzzy longing for his childhood years, the years he had roamed carefree around the village—that is, before his friend, while baiting fish, drowned in the river. His friend with whom he had raided farms and poultry. Jaya had named his son after his friend because he thought that would lessen his guilt.

Clouds were brooding on the horizon.

Jaya closed his eyes to fantasize about what lay ahead. He didn't care if it rained all the way to Zuma Rock. In a few hours, he would check into the hotel his client had paid for. Just one night. Only one night. He would earn an amount he could never make in a month as a plumber. He guessed his client might be about twenty years older. She had described where she lived, an exclusive neighbourhood populated by men and women who had "sucked the country's oil-fat nipples dry." She revealed a lot about her life on WhatsApp. Her husband had died while having sex with an undergraduate student in a hotel in Onitsha, where he had run one of his haulage and logistics companies.

His client liked afang soup with lots of periwinkles and shrimps. She also liked champagne and Congolese music. Papa Wemba and Kofi Olomide were her favourites. Sure, there would be some "crotch-caressing" jigs between them, she had told him. If everything worked out right, he could get used to this kind of job. Give up a life of unclogging stinky drains and having to literally deal with other people's shit.

Jaya jerked awake in his seat at the sound of a door slamming. He had dozed off.

Gazing around, he said, "Where are we?"

Sequinned Jeans told him they were at Agbor Junction.

Craning his neck at the window, Jaya saw the driver at the gas pump cracking walnuts between his teeth. The uniformed attendant gauged his meter.

"See her tiny yansh."

Jaya heard someone titter with glee. He raised his head just in time to see the girl step out of the bus, tugging her pink blouse down over her waist. He noted the exposed curves of her backside and thought of the photos his client had shared with him on WhatsApp before deleting them.

Passengers began filing out of the bus.

"Washroom is over there," yelled the bus driver.

Jaya got out too but lingered around and thought of snacks to buy. It was windy, and he felt it sting his skin. He rubbed his arms and wished he had worn a sweater.

"Lucky her, that's how they go missing," Bearded Man said.

He was the last passenger to step out of the bus.

Jaya spun round to look closely at him, but Bearded Man was squinting up as though he was reading patterns in the greying sky and didn't wish to say anything more. At last, he looked straight into Jaya's eyes—his expression as terse and cryptic as his statement.

"It's going to rain blood," he said, brushing him lightly as he went by.

Jaya stood there for a moment, puzzled. He wondered what his seatmate meant by that. He suspected the man was probably hiding something, or from someone. He had never encountered anyone so strange before.

Twenty minutes later, the driver swerved the bus back onto the road. Only the girl had stayed at Agbor Junction; the other passengers were continuing to Abuja. Mohawk Boy slapped Tattoo Boy on the shoulder, nodding toward the dashboard. Tattoo Boy pleaded with the driver to "pump up the volume." The moment the volume went up, a voice raspy and belligerent hollered from the speakers. The boys whooped with delight, rocking their bodies to the bumpy rhythm.

"Olamide!" they chorused.

Husband and Wife winked at each other.

Sequinned Jeans wiped tears of laughter from her eyes.

Glasses started griping about boys who had gone astray.

Jaya envied the boys for their unconcern.

After the song ended, the boys began arguing about the richest Nigerian artiste—Davido, P-Square, Wizkid, Banky W. Their argument soon veered into the saccharine life their peers led abroad.

"My cousin done hit spicy mama for Canada," Mohawk Boy said.

"You mean MC Vegas? Bastaaard guy! Hope na better spicy mama?" Tattoo Boy said.

"Maami, any spicy mama na spicy mama. So long as you get permanent residence. I show you the video he send me last time?"

"See your goddamn life? When?"

"MC Vegas say filthy rich spicy mamas plenty for Canada dey look for strong black dudes."

"Goddamn bastard. But I hear say the cold in Canada fit shrink man's penis."

They both laughed hard and long like a pair of roadside drunks.

For the next forty minutes, the boys talked about friends who "packaged" girls to Dubai and Oman, where Arab princes doled out dollars to sample black girls. They rattled off the names of foreign cities with fluency.

Jaya wondered how they had come by such information.

Almost everyone listened to the boys. No one cut them short or told them off, only made small, baffled sounds every now and again.

"The boys of nowadays," hissed Sequinned Jeans.

The boys ignored her.

They were in their early twenties, a little younger than Jaya, but the way they boasted of their knowledge made him regret his poor education. The way they extolled, in loud, electric voices, the exploits of Nigerian hackers and scammers (with names such as TTK, Digital, Cyber, and Wireless). The way they bragged about con artists living large in Europe and North America. It all sounded so enticing that Jaya wished again that he wasn't just a struggling plumber.

"That's why Owerri is rotten," Sequinned Jeans muttered, crinkling the corners of her lips. "People like those fraudsters you worship have destroyed *ala* Igbo. Look at the striptease bars everywhere. Look at the number of hotels next door to schools. And that hopeless governor."

Her sense of disapproval must have tainted the driver's mood, for he added tartly, "No one should be surprised if these young men sell their mothers to make wealth."

Tattoo Boy clenched his jaw and cracked his knuckles. He looked like he could punch someone. "What's fucking wrong with taking back the goddamn money white people have stolen from us? Not as if we are into armed robbery or kidnapping."

"*Tufiakwa!* This is a wicked generation," Glasses cried, heaving as if he would burst into coughs. "Men and women trading in the pursuits of the flesh. God's wrath is coming."

"Maami," said Mohawk Boy. "Tell that to politicians who screw the country into the dustbin. Talk from now till Judgement Day, nothing will stop us from Yahoo!-ing." The vehemence in his voice trailed ice through the bus, stopping the conversation from going any further.

Jaya's stomach loosened up now that everyone was quiet. If the vexed chatter had gone on a minute longer, it would have flared into a full-blown quarrel. His hunger returned. He sipped the tepid Sprite he had bought earlier at Agbor Junction. He polished off the biscuits and plantain chips. He then tossed the empty packets into the wastepaper basket in the aisle.

He was picturing himself in bed with his client when he heard the driver announce that the rain was coming. The picture faded, and he saw the clouds had formed a dense grey swell.

"Going to be a heavy one," said Sequinned Jeans. She observed the shadows gathering outside her window. "The type that flooded my village and destroyed my parents' house. People died."

"Which village was that?" asked the driver.

"Obingwa."

"You must have seen the photos of those beautiful homes in Lagos nearly swallowed by floods, yes?" Glasses chuckled. He swept his eyes around to see if anyone nodded their heads. When no one showed interest, he stubbed his finger at his newspaper, whining, "But every newspaper carried the photos on its front page."

Everyone completely ignored him.

In the silence that followed, Jaya sang along with Asa on the radio. He lingered on *"life is short"* and reminded himself to phone his wife once the bus entered the craggy town of Okene. With the fabulous pay he hoped to get from his client, he could make life much easier for everyone. He thought about getting his son one of those colourful toy cars hawked on the streets. He smiled and continued singing.

Something crackled overhead suddenly, causing everyone to flinch in their seats. A cluster of bangs followed.

Jaya was sure that they had run into an ambush this time. Highway robbers. Was this how he was going to die? Oh, God! No. No, not like this. He'd always believed that he would outlive his parents since he was their only child. He couldn't imagine what grief would do to them. To his relief, he realized that the bangs were thunderclaps, and he chided himself for being fearful.

He calmly sat back while swift white light scattered around the bus, setting the air momentarily aglow.

"Lagos will be flooded again." Glasses snickered and waved his folded-up newspaper for emphasis. "That city is going to sink soon."

"Couldn't have come at a better time, God's wrath," Bearded Man told him. "Must be feeling good with yourself, Mr. Newspaper."

"Good, how? I don't understand what you're jabbering about."

"I suggest we share secrets before we part ways. Who wants to go first?"

Everyone stared at Bearded Man in surprise. He had kept much to himself since the trip began several hours ago.

Jaya wasn't as surprised as they were. He and his seatmate had merely passed indirect comments, like the strangers they were. But now, Jaya found it amusing that an exchange was about to happen. He had known all along that there was something mysterious about him.

"Yes, I didn't think so," Bearded Man said. He turned and narrowed his eyes at the boys. "Rangy dogs. You both have runny mouths. Do you mind taking the lead?"

The boys regarded each other with what looked like disbelief. Then they faced Bearded Man and blew up at the same time.

"Look at this moron," Tattoo Boy spoke a little too loudly. "I will smash your goddamn face if you insult us again."

"Watch your mouth, you *ezi*," Mohawk Boy added, clenching his fists, "before I tear it with one blow."

Thunder rumbled just when Bearded Man was about to respond to their threats, and he paused, smiled a razor-thin smile, and looked out the window, probably distracted by the gloom outside.

The dark clouds struck Jaya as too enormous, heaving as if they were climbing down from the sky to devour the road at any minute.

Something crashed on the other side of the road with a heavy thud—the mournful shriek of trees carried over into the bus. The gusty wind pounded itself against the glass and steel.

Jaya clasped his knees and wondered if his seatmate was insane. How could he be smiling on such a stormy journey? Did he not worry that their bus might crash? The highway seemed to be narrowing and undulating—could the driver even see through the quivering dark blur?

"Listen up, brethren!" Bearded Man interjected after a long pause. "The Valley of the Shadow is at hand, so we had better get this charade over with. Mr. Newspaper, you love reading the dailies, right? In a few hours, people will be reading about you."

"Is that a threat?' Glasses frowned. "*Imaonyembu?* You don't even know who I am."

"I don't threaten. I take," Bearded Man replied, then added jokingly, "But my goodness, you're Alexander the Great. Oh, I think you're Napoleon Bonaparte returned from Waterloo."

"You must be sick in the head." Glasses jabbed a finger at him.

Bearded Man gave a laugh, a little hollow laugh, one without feeling.

The couple exchanged uneasy glances, but the boys quietly watched him, smouldering with hate.

"Does anyone wish to know who this nasty piece of mud is?" Bearded man asked no one in particular, though he was nodding at Glasses.

"Hey, watch your language!"

"Or what? I'm not like any of those girls. Remember that girl you got pregnant, the second one who cried at your office desk? Not the younger one you got expelled from the university for alleged exam malpractices. You knew she went to see a quack. Nipped in the bud when she had just begun to blossom. Look, Mr. Newspaper, you go about preying on other people's daughters while you cherish your own, right?"

Glasses dropped his mouth open.

"What's he talking about?" Mohawk Boy asked, looking around.

"Are you a seer or what?" Tattoo Boy scoffed.

"A seer, my foot!" Sequinned Jeans hissed. "He looks like a cheap PI."

"P-what?" Tattoo looked confused.

"Private investigator."

"A private investigator?" Bearded Man blurted, letting his eyes roam up her chest to her face. "In all my journeys, no one has ever called me that. Hmm. That's a new one. Madam Officer, maybe you can say a thing or two about robbery. Are your police killing robbers only to cart away their loot?"

Sequinned Jeans flinched.

Jaya suspected his seatmate had just dug up a long-buried secret.

The other passengers directed their gazes at her.

Sequinned Jeans was silent for a minute or two, and then she straightened her back. In a lower tone, she asked, "Is this some sort of joke?"

"I'm not laughing, as you can see."

Sequinned Jeans scowled at him. "You think this is funny?"

Bearded Man scowled back. "The joke will be on you very soon, Madam Officer. I'm all set to hear how your team butchered the kidnapper whom you'd set up and robbed. For the record, I could go on about what your team did last Christmas Eve, but since my time's almost up, I don't intend to waste it on your deeds."

An ashen look crossed her face.

The exchange no longer amused Jaya. He'd expected excitement, but this was sickening. It felt as though a stranger had shown him his neighbour's underwear. No one spoke now, but the silence didn't cheer him at all. Through the window, he could see that the road had become a swamp—waters swarming the tires as the bus skidded, surged, swerved, and groaned.

The driver kept his eyes on the road, cursing in his local dialect and honking to alert his fellow motorists in the blinding rain. Oncoming vehicles chugged and sputtered past the bus, splashing water against its windows.

For a second, Jaya feared the glass would shatter onto his lap. He expected one or two passengers to caution the driver or protest his reckless driving. Anything could go wrong at this moment. The driver could lose his grip on the steering wheel and crash into an electrical tower. The wind could even fling the bus off the road, upending it. But no one paid him or the driver any attention because Bearded Man had antagonized them.

Jaya felt a pinch in his chest. Was he going to have a heart attack? He tried to control his breathing by thinking about his family. He remembered the Saturdays he chased his son around the soccer field, the evenings he pinched his wife on her backside while she was busy in the kitchen. But he just couldn't slow his breathing because the images of gorges flanking both sides of the road had crowded his head, and his heart was racing faster.

Clutching the edges of his seat with his sweaty hands, Jaya prayed that the driver wouldn't plunge them all into a gorge. He prayed he would escape this nightmare to see his son regain his health.

"Why are you saying all this? You're hurting them, can't you see?" Husband asked Bearded Man.

"Look, it's the lovey-dovey couple. Lovebirds flocking together..." Bearded Man let out a few coos, looking cheerful. Then, turning to stare into Wife's face, he said, "You should know that the man for whom you killed your husband sleeps with your daughter while you're at work. If only you knew how young his niece was when he took her flower, you'd never look at him the same."

Husband tried to protest but burst out coughing. He coughed for about a minute, his head bowed. Patting his chest, he pulled himself together. Still, his voice quavered as he lashed out, "You're lying. You are a bloody liar!"

"Liar, I'm not." Bearded Man shook his head. "Bloody? I could be." He nodded pensively, then yawned. "I can tell you how you're going to die." He turned again to face Wife, who looked already stricken. "Love can take one's limb, so expensive. So how does it feel to have one's husband killed just because one was in love with his best friend? I can tell you what colour of shirt this prick was wearing while he fumbled with your daughter's dress—"

"Leave her alone, you devil!" Husband's face gleamed with sweat.

Wife had slipped into a stream of tears. Husband reached out a hand to pull her over to him. She slapped it away and balled shaky fists to her mouth. He glared at Bearded Man, who simply shrugged.

Jaya felt skittish and considered jumping to the last row. But the crazy wind was lashing at the windows and the door as if trying to fling them open and hurl everyone out into the storm. Jaya stayed back and inched closer to the edge of the seat. He was convinced that his seatmate would scandalize everyone aboard. Would he harm someone physically, too?

The driver flicked a glance over his shoulder. "How come you know so much about other people's business?"

"Everybody's business is my business."

"You're probably no saint yourself."

"Story for the gods. Come on, Mr. Righteous, let's talk about Itu Bridge."

"What happened there?" the driver snapped, banging on the horn.

"You are asking me? Brethren, ask him what happened along Uyo-Calabar road," Bearded Man explained, without even glancing his way. "What a bloody piece of human wreck, but who was at fault? The child, whom you left bleeding on the road after running him over? Or his mother who, ragged and naked, has been wandering the town looking for her son's killer?"

The driver seemed to shrink in his seat.

"Who do you think you are trying to scare?" asked Mohawk Boy, his eyes burning. "Who gives you the right to embarrass and threaten people? I bet you're just as bad as the rest of us."

"My job is not to threaten. I'm only an escort. I report to someone whose paycheck is begotten of blood," Bearded Man said and shot a knowing glance at Jaya, who clenched his jaw and thought it unwise to even challenge him.

"Yes, talking of paychecks," Bearded Man went on. "Sweetness is what brought us here in the first place. Sweetness of the thighs, of bread eaten in secret, so long as one's wife is not in the loop. Sweetness of money taken or stolen in secret, so long as the dead tell no tales. Abuja may not be all sweetness. But even sweetness has poison at its core once you get the hang of it." He tapped his forehead. "I know a son who is left at home to burn in a fever. I know friends who once played on a riverbank and one drowned."

Bearded Man wound his fingers around his throat and began gasping playfully. "I can't breathe, I can't breathe, but I stood there watching the whole time." Then he dropped his hands and began chuckling to himself. "I'm getting ahead of myself, and before I forget... who's next?"

Jaya turned limp and breathless. He tried not to think about his childhood and fought off the guilt that had long clutched his heart. He pried loose the two top buttons on his shirt to let some air into his chest.

"Let's throw this bastard off the bus," Tattoo Boy suggested.

"We can beat you up and no one will do anything," Mohawk Boy threatened, almost lunging at him.

Bearded Man flicked something off his collar, unconcerned, looking like someone used to being threatened. Someone who could never be harmed. He gazed around himself and laughed a horrid laugh.

"Tell me, runny mouths." He slung the words at the boys. "How do you sleep at night with the stench of burning hair? What about the terrible screams he gave before he was charred whole? You couldn't repay the loan you owed him. And when he came banging on your door, threatening to get the police to pick you up, you yelled out to your neighbours that you were being robbed. And together, with the mob you raised, you mauled your partner in crime to death? Run your mouths, why don't you? Run, run, run. You will *taste* the scent of burning flesh before long."

The mortified look in the boys' eyes churned Jaya's stomach. A strange yolk-like taste gripped his throat. He made a retching sound. He spat out on the floor, sprang out of his seat, and tucked himself in the back seat. Jaya wished someone would gag his seatmate and stop him from talking further.

"I wished there was a kinder way to put it," Bearded Man said. "I'm here to escort all but one down the Valley of the Shadow…"

He paused mid-speech because Sequinned Jeans had whipped out a Beretta from nowhere and was pointing it at him. Every other passenger looked horrified. She aimed it straight at his forehead, her eyes enlarged and flaming red.

"Shut up! Just shut up!" she screamed, her arms vibrating.

The driver was swearing and stamping on his brakes.

Everyone but Jaya and Bearded Man had scattered, diving straight under their seats, cradling their heads, and whispering prayers. Petrified, Jaya pictured the bright flash of bullets flying out of the muzzle and ricocheting around the bus, shattering skulls. He couldn't have known that he would end up on a bus full of crazy people, and this could be his last trip. Unless a miracle happened in the next few seconds, he would never see his family ever again.

Until now, Jaya hadn't imagined himself dying in an accident and, worse still, dying when he was only twenty-eight. It dawned on him that no one would recover their bodies if the woman failed to put her gun away right this moment.

Jaya's heart scuttled around his chest like it was scrambling to break free from the jaws of a many-legged creature trapped between the curves of his ribcage. His wife had always told him to take his gut feeling seriously, but he'd had more pressing issues like their sickly child, house rent, and food to worry about. Often, he teased her for being superstitious. He now hated himself for ignoring the sign in the clouds on his way to the bus station that morning.

Jaya regretted having ever phoned his cousin.

"Look, this wasn't how I'd planned it," Bearded Man began to say. "I wanted for most of you an end, so swift, so painless, but this is perfect nonetheless."

In the looming seconds before the ten-seater bus would slam into the shoulder, somersault from the impact, bang its occupants against one another, sling one or two out of their seats and through the splintering windshield—its wheels slicing a body in two and mincing another into the tar—Jaya realized what his friend's final thoughts had been while he had simply stood by watching him thrash under the water's green surface.

Jaya stared unseeing at the metal floor, his heart hammering in his ears. All around him pulsed a deep silence, though distorted, as if he were underwater.

# ACKNOWLEDGEMENTS

This book is a creation of various itineraries and interactions in diverse but inclusive spaces. I am grateful for the generosity of the International Writing Program at the University of Iowa (US), Sanskriti Kendra Foundation (India), Chateau de Lavigny (Switzerland), Civitella Ranieri Foundation (Italy), and the University of Alberta (Canada).

There is no pillar like that of a family. My wife Chioma and our children—Munachimso, Chimdindu, Chiziterem, and Chimdiuto—have supported my creative writing. I appreciate my family for their love, patience, and understanding, especially when I am struggling to shape or finish a story. Special thanks to my mom, Rhoda; sisters—Kome, Rita, Kate, and Gift, and my in-laws—Mr. and Mrs. Rufus Ali, Iwuchukwu, Chizoba, Tunji, Nnedi, Ifeanyi, and Emeka.

My amazing editors, Kara Toews and 'Tayo Keyede, for their multiple edits of the early draft. Thanks also to Kimmy Beach and Laura Osgood for their incredible editorial support. Each of these people guided me with valuable feedback throughout the revision process. Thanks also to Lahoucine Ouzgane, Chielozona Eze, Isidore Diala, and Kevin Hutchings for offering me unstinting support when I needed it the most, especially during the days my writing seemed like a struggle.

My warm thanks to the friendship of writers who read rough versions of the stories, namely—Okey Ndibe, E.C. Osondu, Ikhide Ikheloa, Helon Habila, Chika Unigwe, Myles Ojabo, Yejide Kilanko, Ukamaka Olisakwe, Abubakar Adam Ibrahim, Chigbo Arthur Anyaduba, Henrietta Rose-Innes, Unoma Azuah, Bruce Cook, Peter Midgley, Matthew Tétreault, and Wendy McGrath.

Nnenna Onuegbu, thank you too. There are many other people whose names I wish I could add here, but I am grateful nonetheless for their kindness during the process of bringing my book to the world.

I salute my publisher, Griots Lounge Publishing, for believing in this book, even when I was not quite sure of it myself. Thank you, Bibi Ukonu, Jide Aluka, and Adaobi Ukonu!

Finally, thank you, dear reader for travelling with me.

*Daalu ndi nke m.*

# BLURBS

"Umezurike's stories are full of wondrous gifts: a poet's ear for language, a depth of insight into the souls of memorable characters straining against often implacable fate and other forces, and a propulsive energy that keeps the reader riveted. He's a delight to discover!"

— Okey Ndibe, author of *Foreign Gods, Inc.*

"These stories make you catch your breath. The characters are so out there, yet so immediate, and their lives buzz with a kind of high-wire tension that keeps you wondering 'What next? Whatever next?' It is a remarkable book."

— Alice Major, author of *Welcome to the Anthropocene.*

"With playful, vivid language, these vibrant stories capture the dreamlike—sometimes nightmarish—poetry of the everyday. A captivating read."

— Henrietta Rose-Innes, author of *Nineveh*

"This bristling collection of short stories had me entirely riveted and struck by their crafted imagery and bold emotional complexity. Several stories have young first-person narrators haunted by relatives now distressingly absent due to social breakage or illness, or whose parents are ferociously present, intrusive, needing to pass on a habit of masculinity as brutality. Others set in the third person introduce couples, neighbours, scam artists and competitors playing out schisms of distrust and self-protection, in concrete village/urban settings fueled by fantastic dialogue and a constant electric edge of the intimate body held in its own defense. A wonderful, impressive read."

— Margaret Christakos, author of *Dear Birch.*

"*Double Wahala, Double Trouble* does everything a work of fiction should do—shock and impress at the same time. Each story here is beautifully crafted, with characters that will linger in the reader's mind long after the reading. Umezurike is a writer with a bright future."

— Helon Habila, author of *Travellers*

"Each of Umezurike's stories leads the reader down a comfortable path, until it is abruptly uncomfortable. His consistent skill in twisting plot lines and the driving needs of his characters is rare in short story collections, no matter where they take place. Lost family, betrayals, the idea—and illusion—of home, and grand, fierce gestures of love flow through this book. Reader: let these outstanding stories wash over you."

— Kimmy Beach, author of *Nuala: A Fable*

*Double Wahala, Double Trouble* is a poetic, gripping, mesmerizing, inventive, and deeply entertaining collection of short stories that cracks open a world that is hidden in the darkest corners of everyday human life. These stories convey Umezurike's brilliance in building suspense and his great vision in exploring complex moral issues of love, identity, family, human relations, memory, and dislocation.

— Niq Mhlongo, author of *Paradise in Gaza*

"In these compelling stories, Umezurike limns the lives of ordinary people trying to survive whichever way they can. Whether he is writing about a lover who makes a disturbing and unexpected sacrifice to secure her love or a man who loses his life

in a case of mistaken identity, Umezurike's prose shines like something very carefully polished."
— Chika Unigwe, author of *Better Never Than Late*

At once funny and painfully real, *Double Wahala, Double Trouble* shows that Umezurike has mastered the art of subtly capturing the nuances of domestic brutality in sparse yet resonant prose. A masterfully delivered collection.
—Abubakar Adam Ibrahim, author of
*Dreams and Assorted Nightmares*

"These are stories with heft, powerfully told. When you leave these stories, the stories don't leave you."
—E.C. Osondu, author of *Alien Stories.*

*Double Wahala, Double Trouble* tells stories of love, pain, and compassion in a broken world. Under the deft hand of Umezurike, it is clear humanity faces a bleak future unless we address the terrible legacies of colonialism, war, and toxic masculinity.
— Peter Midgley, author of *let us not think of them as barbarians*

Umezurike's stories exhibit a range of events, from everyday breakups to rebel military clashes to small-time, small-town opportunists. But at the heart of these stories is the breakdown of relationships, particularly between parents and children. Umezurike has portrayed a world in which too often pride and self-doubt cloud the decisions of adults who shape the futures of their children. The effect on the characters is sometimes baffling, sometimes humorous, often tragic; in these stories, everyone is a victim of someone else's yearnings. Certainly, there are big yearnings in this collection. But Umezurike's clear strength is his ability to show how even the smallest yearning can also be a big wahala.
— Bertrand Bickersteth, author of *The Response of Weeds*

In prose as lucid as it is engaging, Umezurike plumbs the lives of the marginalized to uncover stories of love, greed, disloyalty, violence, rejection, family, and nationhood. Umezurike shows us ordinary people caught up in extraordinary circumstances, people struggling to remain human in our often-cruel world. *Double Wahala, Double Trouble* is a stupendous collection, offering delightfully delicious fare for its readers.

—Jeffery Renard Allen, author of *Song of the Shank*

These stories linger long after they've been read. They bite, shock, and titillate! A great addition to the genre of the short story, and a welcoming one.

—Vamba Sherif, author of *The Black Napoleon*

These stories were previously published in a different form: "Bat" in *Maple Tree Literary Supplement;* "Journey" in *Evergreen Review;* "Neighbours" in *The Lamp;* "Double Wahala" in *Works in Progress and Other Stories;* "Stupid" in *The North East Review;* "Wild Flames" in *Dream Chasers* and *Author Africa;* and "Move On" in *Sleeping Fish.*

# ABOUT THE AUTHOR

**UCHECHUKWU PETER UMEZURIKE** holds a PhD in English from the University of Alberta. A poet, fiction writer, essayist, and literary journalist, he is a recipient of the James Patrick Folinsbee Memorial Scholarship in Creative Writing from the University of Alberta and the Norma Epstein Foundation Award for Creative Writing from the University of Toronto, among many honours. He is a co-editor of *Wreaths for a Wayfarer,* an anthology of poems. His children's book, *Wish Maker,* is forthcoming from Masobe Books in the fall of 2021. He lives in Edmonton, Alberta.